"When were you [going to tell me]
I have a daughter.[..]"

Sarah stared at him, not knowing what to say.

"You *weren't*." Jace breathed into the silence. "You were going to let me leave..."

"You did before, knowing that...you could be a father." Sarah hated that her voice came out low, shaky, but Jace flinched.

"Addie is my child, Sarah. You didn't think I had a right to know?"

"A right?" she echoed. "You left, Jace. And you never called. Never came back. You made a life and so did I. Don't question the decision I made because *you* made one first."

Sarah was surprised at the bitterness in her voice.

She had forgiven him and yet she couldn't erase the past. Jace Marshall had broken her heart, but Sarah had to protect Addie's. Ten years may have gone by, but that didn't mean he'd changed.

And he proved it when he turned and strode out of the barn.

Kathryn Springer is a lifelong Wisconsin resident. Growing up in a "newspaper" family, she spent long hours as a child plunking out stories on her mother's typewriter and hasn't stopped writing since. She loves to write inspirational romance because it allows her to combine her faith in God with her love of a happy ending.

Books by Kathryn Springer

Love Inspired

The Secret She Kept

Castle Falls

The Bachelor Next Door
The Bachelor's Twins
The Bachelor's Perfect Match
The Holiday Secret

Mirror Lake

A Place to Call Home
Love Finds a Home
The Prodigal Comes Home
Longing for Home
The Promise of Home
Making His Way Home

Visit the Author Profile page at LoveInspired.com for more titles.

THE SECRET
SHE KEPT

KATHRYN SPRINGER

LOVE INSPIRED
INSPIRATIONAL ROMANCE

If you purchased this book without a cover you should be aware
that this book is stolen property. It was reported as "unsold and
destroyed" to the publisher, and neither the author nor the
publisher has received any payment for this "stripped book."

LOVE INSPIRED®
INSPIRATIONAL ROMANCE

Recycling programs
for this product may
not exist in your area.

ISBN-13: 978-1-335-93721-6

The Secret She Kept

Copyright © 2025 by Kathryn Springer

All rights reserved. No part of this book may be used or reproduced in any
manner whatsoever without written permission.

Without limiting the author's and publisher's exclusive rights, any
unauthorized use of this publication to train generative artificial intelligence
(AI) technologies is expressly prohibited.

This is a work of fiction. Names, characters, places and incidents are either the
product of the author's imagination or are used fictitiously. Any resemblance
to actual persons, living or dead, businesses, companies, events or locales is
entirely coincidental.

For questions and comments about the quality of this book, please contact us
at CustomerService@Harlequin.com.

® is a trademark of Harlequin Enterprises ULC.

Love Inspired
22 Adelaide St. West, 41st Floor
Toronto, Ontario M5H 4E3, Canada
www.LoveInspired.com

Printed in Lithuania

MIX
Paper | Supporting
responsible forestry
FSC® C021394

Trust in the Lord with all thine heart;
and lean not unto thine own understanding.
In all thy ways acknowledge him,
and he shall direct thy paths.
—*Proverbs* 3:5–6

This book is lovingly dedicated to
my granddaughters, Cassidy, Evelyn, Fiona, Tabitha
and Beatrice. For all the sweet memories we've
made so far and the many adventures yet to come!

Chapter One

Jace Marshall's duffel bag hit the tile floor with a soft thud as he reached into his mailbox and began to thumb through the contents.

Credit card applications. Outdated sale catalogs from home-improvement and sporting-goods stores.

A travel brochure promising sunshine and sand.

His lips twisted.

Thanks, but no thanks.

Jace had had his fill of both the past eighteen months.

"I thought I heard the door open." Dorothea Blumberg waved to him from the landing at the top of the stairs.

The events on the world stage might change daily, but there were two constants in the three-story Victorian where Jace rented a room—his landlady's sharp ears and her ability to avoid every loose board and weak spot that gave her position away. If Dorothea were forty years younger, Jace would have welcomed her on his team.

"Nice to see you, Mrs. B."

"You're too thin."

Never mind that his weight hadn't changed since the last time he'd been on leave. Or the time before that. Dorothea's solution was always the same.

"Lasagna," she declared. "There's an extra pan in the freezer. I'll drop it off before *Jeopardy!*"

There was no point in arguing. Not that Jace would. After

weeks of MREs, there were nights he'd dreamed about Mrs. B's lasagna.

He sorted through the rest of the mail, the pile dwindling quickly as he fired the majority of it into the recycling bin conveniently located underneath the row of mailboxes in the foyer. A white envelope trapped between a glossy flyer advertising a new fitness center and a coupon book from a local grocery store slipped free and fluttered to the floor. Jace reached down and scooped it up—and froze when he saw the familiar logo stamped above the return address.

Four Arrows Camp.

His pulse began to hammer even though he had no idea what was inside.

Jace hadn't heard from Maggie Malone, the camp director, in years.

"Jace?"

He tore his gaze from the envelope. Dorothea had returned. She leaned over the railing, jewel-encrusted reading glasses dancing from the ends of the gold chain fastened around her neck. "I forgot to say welcome home."

Home.

The first-floor studio apartment overlooking Dorothea's rose garden was clean and comfortable but to Jace, it was merely a place to crash between deployments.

The closest he'd come to having a home was the address written on the back of the envelope clutched in his hand.

"Thanks, Mrs. B." Jace forced a smile and tucked the envelope in his pocket before shouldering his duffel bag and heading down the hall.

He let himself into the apartment and the scent of lemon furniture polish stung his nose. His landlady waged a daily war against any dust particles that dared to accumulate in the house. When Dorothea found out Jace was in the service, she'd insisted that he let her keep his rooms "tidy" when he was away, before she handed over the lease.

Jace had agreed, of course. He'd needed an apartment and truth be told, there wasn't much to dust around. Almost everything he owned fit in the bag that he tossed on the couch. He sank down beside it and fanned out the rest of the mail on the mirrored surface of the mahogany coffee table.

Okay. Not all of it.

He was still ignoring the envelope in his pocket, afraid that once he broke the seal, he would be overpowered by a flood of memories.

Why would Maggie be writing to him now?

Ten years ago, at the request of a pastor who'd volunteered at Four Arrows, the camp director had thrown out a lifeline to Jace and two other kids who'd aged out of foster care. Not only had Maggie generously offered them a place to live that summer, she'd provided some breathing room. Guidance. Time and space and a little hard work while they figured out their next step.

No matter how hard Jace had tried, it had been impossible to keep his distance from Maggie. She was like everyone's favorite TV mom. Patient. Wise. Funny. And unlike a lot of the people in Jace's life up to that point, Maggie didn't seem to care about the mile-long list of flaws and failures that had followed Jace from foster home to foster home like a shadow.

It was Maggie who'd challenged and encouraged him. Told him that he had a Father who loved him and would never leave. Something Jace's own dad had sure never modeled. Because Maggie had lived like she believed it was true, Jace had started to read the Bible she'd stowed in his backpack before he'd left. And, blown away by the fact that God loved him in spite of all his mistakes, he'd taken that first stumbling step forward in His direction and believed it, too.

Jace probably should have told Maggie he'd become a Christian a long time ago. Maybe it was time to let her know that all the prayers she'd said on his behalf hadn't gone unanswered.

There'd been a good reason why he hadn't contacted her, hadn't responded to the letter she'd sent while he was in boot camp, but regret pressed down hard.

Time to rectify one of his mistakes.

Jace pulled the envelope from his pocket and tore open the flap.

The wrinkled index card inside stirred another memory and Jace smiled as it took shape.

It had been his last night at the camp and Rae Channing had cornered Jace and Ian in the cook shack, where they'd been assigned to dish duty after lunch.

"Maggie has done so much for us this summer," she'd said. "I think we should do something special for her."

"Like what?" Ian had been a just-the-facts kind of guy. "We don't have any money to buy Maggie a gift. We don't have, well, anything."

True. But Rae hadn't backed down.

"Someday we'll have something, though," she'd persisted, a fiery determination blazing in her eyes that dared Jace and Ian—or anyone else—to contradict her. "Why don't we give her a…a promise? If Maggie ever needs help, no matter what, no matter when, all she has to do is let us know and we'll come back."

It had sounded kind of lame to Jace, not to mention a little risky, but Maggie would probably like it. She had been into the whole helping people sort of thing.

"We'll each give her a card and sign it, so she won't forget." Rae had already opened a drawer by the sink, looking for paper. Her search produced three index cards and a stub of a pencil with no eraser. She handed one of the cards to Jace and he'd looked at it doubtfully.

"What am I supposed to write?"

Rae had chewed on her bottom lip. "One wish," she'd finally said. "We'll explain what they're for when she reads them."

Jace had glanced at Ian, expecting the guy would come up with another question. Or a list of reasons why a someday promise wouldn't begin to cover everything Maggie Malone had done for them over the past twelve weeks.

"I made a wooden box during arts and crafts time," Ian had said instead. "We can put the notes in that and give it to her at Campfire tonight."

Jace's heart had knocked against his sternum.

Sarah would be at the campfire...

An image of a heart-shaped face, strawberry blond hair and fern-green eyes flashed in Jace's mind before he could stop it. He hadn't thought about Sarah Crosse in years.

Hadn't *let* himself think about her.

When Jace had agreed to spend the summer in The Middle of Nowhere, Wisconsin, he'd had no idea he would meet a girl like Sarah. Sweet. Stunning.

Totally out of his league.

But that hadn't stopped Jace from seeking her out on the days she'd volunteered...

Jace yanked his thoughts back in line.

Nope. Not going there.

Sarah was part of Jace's past and her future hadn't included a guy like him.

Something Dr. Crosse, Sarah's father, had bluntly pointed out when he'd cornered Jace at the camp one afternoon.

And because Jace knew it was true, he'd done the right thing for once.

That had been Maggie's influence, too.

Jace stared down at the card, surprised and a little amused the camp director had kept the coupon for over a decade.

The words *one wish* were printed in large, blocky letters that looked like a kindergartener practicing his penmanship.

And at the bottom of the paper…
Something Jace didn't remember writing at all.
Please come as soon as you can. We need help.

The thunderstorm that had rolled through the county right before dawn had littered the grounds with branches and pine-cones before it moved on.

Sarah would have to deal with that later.

Right now, she was staring at the debris field left by a ten-year-old tornado named Addie as she'd spun through the kitchen in her haste to eat breakfast. A rule Sarah had implemented before her daughter was allowed to visit the barn in the morning.

Star, her daughter's four-legged best friend and confidante, wasn't a fan of thunderstorms, so Sarah knew that Addie would be anxious to check on her.

She put the carton of milk back in the refrigerator and cleaned up the trail of crumbs and blobs of strawberry jam that started at the toaster and ended at the ceramic fruit bowl by the coffee pot. The apples she'd bought at the store the day before were gone. All that was left was one overripe banana.

Sarah didn't want to scold Addie for feeding her snack to the horses, but their grocery budget was tight.

Oh, who was she kidding? Everything was tight.

Four Arrows' success depended on an army of loyal volunteers, both from Crosse Creek Community, a local church that understood the importance of Maggie's ministry, and the people who'd spent a summer there as campers or counselors and wanted to give back to the camp that had changed their lives.

Jean and Bob Hoffman were the latter. The couple had supported Four Arrows for years. Jean, a retired hospital dietician, supervised the cafeteria while her husband took care of everything from maintaining the grounds to capturing and relocating the occasional critter—flying or crawling—that found its way into a cabin.

Sarah had been happy to see Jean's name pop up on the screen of her cell phone…until she'd broken the news that Sarah would have to find someone else to take their place this summer. Their daughter, who lived out of state, had been diagnosed with preeclampsia, so Jean and Bob would be moving in to help with the older children until the baby was born.

Sarah had understood. Family came first. But right now, she had to face the fact that there might not *be* another summer.

Finding last-minute replacements for Jean and Bob would be difficult enough, but two unexpected cancellations from some of their regulars would result in a loss of income that Sarah wasn't sure they could bounce back from. Generous endowments from former alumni kept Four Arrows afloat during the winter months, but the income from the campers was crucial in order to meet the day-to-day expenses.

If Maggie were here, she would know what to do.

Sarah might have called Four Arrows home for the past ten years, but Maggie was the one who'd founded it. Understood the ins and outs of running a camp. Organized the volunteers and balanced the budget.

Sarah was the resident wrangler. She spent more time with horses than people and preferred it that way.

For Maggie's sake—and Addie's—she was trying, though.

Four Arrows was the only home her daughter had ever known, and Sarah didn't want to let her down, either.

Sarah's breath tumbled out in a sigh, but the ache that had settled in her chest didn't ease. After talking to Jean, she'd contacted a local catering company and was waiting to find out if they could spare an employee who could plan and prepare meals for both the campers and some of the special events on the summer schedule.

The only payment Bob and Jean had ever accepted was the use of a private cabin for the summer. Hiring a cook would take a large chunk from the camp's already tight budget. A chunk they couldn't afford.

There was a way to keep the camp solvent, but Sarah knew it would break her daughter's heart...

"Mom?" Addie's breathless voice floated through the screen door. "Someone's at the lodge."

Sarah frowned.

The main lodge housed a common gathering room where campers checked in to register, Maggie's office, the infirmary, and a nook stocked with snacks and souvenirs affectionately known as the General Store. Two of the rooms on the second floor were designated for storage, but Maggie had converted the rest of the space into an apartment.

As the director, Sarah couldn't avoid the building, but the air was crowded with memories, making it difficult to linger there now that her friend and mentor was gone.

The regular delivery drivers bypassed the lodge and drove straight to the cabin that Sarah shared with Addie whenever they had to drop off a package, but it was early in the season. Someone new might not realize that Sarah wasn't keeping regular office hours yet.

She stepped onto the narrow porch and felt the warm caress of the sun on her face. So far, the temperature had been above normal for the first week of June, a blessing after a winter that had finally, reluctantly, released its grip on the Northwoods.

A black pickup truck Sarah didn't recognize was parked in front of the lodge. Addie had returned to the stable and Sarah could hear her singing along with Maggie's ancient CD player, a lively praise song that made Sarah smile.

She was still smiling when she walked up the driveway and saw the man blocking the welcome sign on the door. His back was to Sarah, but gray cargo pants and a black, long-sleeved T-shirt emphasized broad shoulders and a lean, athletic frame.

Sarah slowed her steps.

At one point, Maggie had talked about installing a security system, but with every penny accounted for, it wasn't high on Sarah's list of priorities anymore.

"Can I help you?"

The man turned and the air emptied from her lungs.

The stunned look on Jace Marshall's face told Sarah that he hadn't expected to see her, either.

While Jace had waited for Maggie to answer the door, bits and pieces of memories began to break free from the walls he'd built around them.

Four Arrows had been both an oasis and a shelter the summer he'd turned eighteen. There'd been laughter and friendships forged around late-night campfires. A girl who'd held his hand and whispered that he could be anything in a soft, lyrical voice Jace still heard occasionally in his dreams.

When he heard that voice again, Jace thought his mind was playing tricks on him, but then the years melted away when he turned around.

Sarah.

Her hair was shorter than he remembered, the contours of her face more defined, enhancing wide green eyes that had seen something in Jace no one else had ever seen. Not even himself.

"What are you doing here?"

They spoke at the same time but neither one of them laughed. Laugh? Jace could hardly breathe.

But…why was Sarah here? At the camp? She should have finished med school and had her own practice by now.

Sarah glanced over her shoulder, unclipped a ring of keys from the carabiner on the belt loop of her faded jeans and opened the door.

Jace took it as an invitation and followed her inside. He'd always loved the main lodge. Built from hand-peeled logs and river rock, the lodge was warm and rustic, yet there was a touch of whimsy in the yellow floor tiles and the colorful mural made up of handprints from the campers who'd gathered there over the years.

His gaze traveled around the spacious room. There were no lights on, which struck him as odd. The sconces that flanked the fireplace had always glowed in welcome, no matter what time of the day or night.

"What are you doing here?" Sarah repeated.

The edge in her voice was different, too, not that Jace could blame her. They hadn't parted on the best of terms. Probably because the last time they'd spoken, Jace had bluntly informed Sarah that he'd already planned out his future and she wasn't part of it.

That she hadn't argued, had let him walk away so easily, had hurt almost as much as the lie.

"I came to see Maggie. Is she here?"

The color drained from Sarah's face, making her eyes appear even larger. "Maggie? No." Her throat convulsed. "She… she passed away three years ago, Jace."

Sarah's lips continued to move but the rushing sound in Jace's ears drowned out everything else out.

Maggie. Gone.

"She can't be." Jace reached into his back pocket, pulled out his wallet and produced the card that had brought him here.

"I got this in the mail."

"One wish." Sarah's lips shaped the words but her voice barely broke a whisper.

"I gave it to Maggie the night…" Another memory Jace had spent ten years trying to forget crashed over him. "The night before I left."

Sarah's eyes darkened and Jace realized she hadn't forgotten, either. Or forgiven him.

Guilt sliced deep even as Jace struggled to wrap his head around the fact that Maggie had passed away. Three *years* ago.

"Did you send this?"

Sarah flinched. *"No."*

"Then who—"

Jace didn't get to finish the question. The door swung open and a girl bounded in, copper ponytail swinging. Her lively, brown-eyed gaze bounced from Sarah to Jace. She spotted the card in Jace's hand and squealed.

"You're here!" She clapped her hands. "I knew you'd come! Are you Mr. Ian? Or Mr. Jace?"

He hadn't thought about Ian Bradford in years. The two of them had nothing in common except for the fact that they'd both been sucked into foster care at a young age and spat out at eighteen. Ian was studious and a little awkward. While Jace had pushed against everything and everyone, Ian had played chameleon. Quiet. Blending in with his surroundings.

"Jace," he answered, bemused by the fact that unlike Sarah, the girl seemed happy to see him. Seemed to have been... expecting him?

"I'm Addie." She danced back to Sarah and grinned up at her. "I told you not to worry, Mom! Isn't this great?"

For the second time in the space of five minutes, Jace felt like he'd been hit with an IED.

Mom.

He cut a glance at Sarah and felt another direct hit as she drew the girl—her *daughter*—against her side almost protectively.

Well, if Jace ever wondered if Sarah had moved on after he'd left, the answer was obvious now. And considering the girl's age, which he guessed to be about eight or nine, she sure hadn't wasted any time replacing him, either.

Chapter Two

*A*ddison Crosse.

What did you do?

Sarah wanted to howl the words. Grab her daughter by the hand and run out the door.

But her feet remained riveted in place.

Eyes the same rich shade of chocolate brown as Addie's locked with Sarah's.

Jace had always been good at hiding his emotions, but the flash of betrayal when Sarah expected to see recognition upset her equilibrium all over again.

Just who had betrayed who?

Jace had broken up with *her*. Left without a backward glance—or forwarding address. Not that Sarah would have contacted him. She'd wanted him to stay out of love, not obligation.

Sarah might have made a mistake by giving Jace Marshall her heart that summer, but she'd vowed to protect her daughter's, no matter what the cost. And the cost *had* been high. But so, so worth it. Jace had left to make his mark on the world but Sarah couldn't imagine a world without Addie.

A world her daughter had unwittingly upended when she'd somehow tracked Jace down and sent the card that had summoned him back to Four Arrows.

Heart still pounding, she slid her gaze to Addie.

"Have you taken the dog for her walk?" Sarah struggled to keep her voice even.

"Not yet. I was feeding Star." Addie bounced up on her toes and turned the full force of her gamine grin on Jace. "She's my horse. Do you want to meet—"

"Addie," Sarah interrupted, her throat constricting again. "You can turn the horses out, too." Spring weather could be volatile, so she'd rounded up the small herd and tucked them into their stalls for the night before the storm had hit. "I'll be there in a few minutes."

Hopefully, it wouldn't take more than that to convince Jace there was no reason for him to stay.

"Okay!" Addie flashed another grin at Jace before the door closed behind her, leaving Sarah alone with…a stranger.

She hadn't realized that her memory of Jace Marshall, like the summer they'd met, had remained frozen in time.

Now, she tried to reconcile this man's clean-shaven jaw, close-cropped hair and confident bearing with the Jace she'd fallen for. At eighteen, Jace had been as lean as a coyote and just as wary, with a shock of dark hair that dipped over his eyes and a smile so rare that it felt like a gift every time Sarah managed to coax one out of him.

She realized he was staring at her, too, and fought the urge to comb her fingers through her hair.

What did he see?

A practical hairstyle more suited to ponytails and baseball caps than curling irons and visits to a salon? The tiny lines fanning out from her eyes that had appeared after Maggie's death?

Or did he see the girl he'd left behind? The girl whose eyes had lit up like Addie's whenever he walked into the room.

The girl who'd kept a secret for ten years and wasn't prepared to answer questions now that he'd shown up out of the blue.

But the only thing Jace asked was "How?"

It took her a moment to realize he was asking about Maggie.

Was it really possible Jace didn't realize that the child who'd sent out an SOS without Sarah's consent—or knowledge—was his daughter, too?

Hope crept in, making it a little easier to breathe.

"An aneurysm." Sarah instinctively wrapped her arms around her middle, shoring up her heart against the memory of that day. "I'd dropped Addie off at school and when I got back, Maggie wasn't in her office. I went upstairs to check on her and…" A lump swelled in Sarah's throat. "She was already gone."

The next few weeks had been a blur. Maggie had been the only child of parents who'd married later in life. Both had passed away and Maggie had never married or had children of her own. Four Arrows was her life, her family made up of the campers, staff and volunteers. They'd all loved Maggie, but it had fallen on Sarah to make the arrangements while grieving the loss of the woman who'd offered her a safe haven, a home, after her father's ultimatum.

A home they could still lose if Sarah didn't turn things around.

"I can't believe it," Jace muttered. "She was what…fifty-five?"

"Almost." She and Addie had been planning Maggie's birthday party.

"She wrote to me once," Jace said. "But…"

His voice trailed off, but Sarah filled in the blank.

She'd had no idea that Maggie had tried to contact Jace, but it didn't surprise her that he hadn't responded. He'd told Sarah that he wanted to leave the past behind. It was her fault she hadn't realized that included her until it was too late.

Jace glanced at the card in his hand. "Your daughter sent this?"

Sarah wished she could deny it, but Addie's enthusiastic reaction to Jace's presence had given her away.

"A few weeks ago, I discovered a bin filled with some of Maggie's things in the attic," she said carefully, not mentioning the reason she'd gone up there in the first place. The ceiling tiles in a corner of the upstairs hallway were damp and Sarah had been trying to find where the leak had originated. "Addie saw the wooden box with the cards inside when I brought the bin downstairs and wanted to know what they were for.

"I—I told her that Maggie had let three teenagers who needed a home stay here one summer, and they gave her coupons good for one wish in case she ever needed them."

"You're telling me that she tracked us down on her own?" A hint of disbelief crept into Jace's voice, but Sarah knew how determined Addie could be.

A trait she and her father had in common.

"Addie asked if she could have the box but I had no idea she'd kept the cards." *Or that she would try to find you.*

"I can't believe Maggie still had them." Jace raked his hand through his hair, a gesture so familiar that Sarah was transported back in time.

She'd been at Campfire the night they'd presented her with the gift. Had seen the tears in Maggie's eyes after she opened it. The shy, self-conscious smile on Jace's face when Maggie had hugged him. The sweet gesture, one that proved Jace wasn't the troublemaker that her father claimed he was, had made Sarah fall even harder.

Looking back, she should have refused his invitation to go for a walk after the fire went out, but Jace was leaving the next day. Sarah had wanted to spend every moment with him. Dream about their future...

She'd been so naive. But not anymore.

"I'm sorry you found out about Maggie like this," Sarah murmured. And she was. No matter how Jace had felt about her, he'd respected Maggie. "I'm sorry you came all this way, too."

Really sorry.

But life was difficult enough at the moment, and Sarah didn't need the added complication of Jace Marshall.

"What she—Addie—wrote," Jace said slowly. "'Please come as soon as you can. We need your help.' Is that true?"

Sarah managed a shaky laugh. "Running a camp always has its challenges, but things are okay." It wasn't a lie because she did *not* need Jace's help.

He didn't look convinced.

Sarah took a step toward the door. A not-so-subtle hint that she didn't have time to take a detour down memory lane. Especially since Addie would cruise through the tasks she'd been assigned and return at any moment.

But Jace didn't move. "Who's the camp director now?"

"I am." Maybe the more times she said it out loud, the more she would feel like one.

"You?"

Sarah didn't know whether to be amused or offended at the shocked expression on Jace's face.

"I know the basics of running a camp."

She just wasn't as good at it as Maggie had been. Not by a long shot. Sarah preferred horses and quiet trail rides through the woods over the hustle and bustle of the main camp.

"But…you're a doctor."

Sarah's heart bottomed out. That dream had died a long time ago. If it had been her dream at all. Her father was the one who'd encouraged her to follow in his footsteps. Go to med school and eventually take over his practice in Crosse Creek after he retired.

"I've been the resident wrangler here for…a long time," she replied. The less Jace knew about her, the better. "I know Maggie would appreciate that you came back, Jace, but we're fine. Really. Everything is under control."

She couldn't make it any clearer than that.

And the Jace Marshall she knew would nod and walk out of her life without a backward glance, the way he'd done ten years ago.

The door flung open so abruptly the pendant light on the ceiling began to sway.

"Mom! You have to come quick!" Addie gasped the words. "A tree fell on the fence in the back pasture."

The ramifications of the announcement tumbled like dominoes through Sarah's mind.

"Did you turn out the horses yet?"

Addie nodded, her eyes wide with panic. "Right before I walked Maisey. And I didn't see them by the barn when we came back."

Can this day get any worse, Lord?

Sarah cast a quick look at Jace as she strode toward the door. "I'm sorry, but if I don't fix the fence, I'll have fifteen horses roaming the woods between here and Crosse Creek."

If they weren't already.

The back pasture was the herd's favorite destination, especially now that the grass had started to grow. Sarah's new goal was to get there first.

The scent of rain still lingered in the air as Sarah took the steps two at a time, Addie at her heels.

"Grab a bucket of grain and some lead ropes," Sarah instructed.

Addie streaked ahead of her without a word, and veered toward the barn.

"We can take my truck."

Sarah hadn't realized Jace was following her.

"Too muddy this time of year." She headed toward the detached garage. "I'll have to use the ATV."

If she could get it started. And people thought horses were unpredictable. Sarah would trust Autumn, her red roan, over a temperamental engine any day.

"I'll come with you."

For a split second, relief poured through Sarah. For the last three years, she'd been doing everything alone. It was so tempting to accept his offer, but the longer Jace stayed, the more questions he might ask. Questions Sarah didn't want to answer.

"There isn't room," she told him. "And you don't have to—"

Jace stopped her with a single look before he cut to the left and disappeared down the wooded trail behind the barn.

The North Path was no longer marked with a sign, but Maggie had put Jace on firewood-collection duty shortly after he'd arrived at the camp. He'd explored every inch of these woods until he was as familiar with the terrain as the horses Sarah was worried would escape.

Jace's boots slipped on the mud—Sarah hadn't been exaggerating—but he jogged down the narrow path, dodging tree limbs and roots protruding from the ground.

A spot of color caught his eye as Jace grabbed a low-hanging branch to steady himself. A bright yellow rock was half buried in the decaying vegetation. It looked so out of place that Jace reached down and picked it up. He scraped the dirt away with the pad of his thumb. Saw the word *trust* written in permanent marker.

One of the campers must have lost it. Jace slipped the rock into his pocket and continued on. When he reached the back pasture, the first thing he spotted was Sarah's daughter and a black-and-white border collie. They were standing guard in front of a gaping hole in the fence but there wasn't a horse in sight.

Had they already discovered the opening and scattered into the woods?

The low growl of an engine grew louder and an ATV rolled between the trees on the opposite side of the pasture. Sarah looked even more petite sitting in the driver's seat of the rust-pocked vehicle. Her jeans were spattered with mud, her hair in disarray from navigating the twists and turns of the trail.

Sarah. Running Four Arrows. She should be wearing scrubs and a stethoscope, not denim and flannel.

And although she'd claimed everything was under control, the subtle changes Jace had seen so far—the blistered paint on some of the cabins, the rotten boards in the steps leading up to the lodge, the fence that should have been replaced long before it crumpled under the weight of a sapling birch—was evidence that Sarah was either lying to him…or to herself.

"Mom!" Sarah's daughter waved as the ATV rolled to a stop near the fallen tree. "The horses went down to the pond instead. I counted and they're all there."

The tension in Sarah's shoulders eased as she hopped down from the vehicle.

One crisis averted.

Thank You, Lord.

The silent prayer slipped out with Jace's next breath.

Maggie would love to know that the kid who'd refused to talk to anyone about his feelings kept up a running conversation with God now.

There was a time Jace was pretty sure that God viewed him the same way everyone else did. Not worthy of His attention. Unfortunately, it was during that time he'd met Sarah.

Smart. Sweet. Beautiful.

She was also an honor roll student—and the only child of a doctor—with an optimistic way of looking at the world that had both challenged and mystified Jace.

You've already had a negative influence on my daughter. Sarah is getting behind on the college prep courses she's taking this summer. She spends all her time here, when she should be studying. But I suppose that doesn't matter to someone like you.

Ten years had gone by, but Dr. Crosse's words still echoed in Jace's head.

It was the "someone like you" that had hit Jace the hardest.

He hadn't bothered to defend himself. Sarah's father wouldn't have cared that Jace was thinking about a career in the military. Wouldn't have believed he could make it through basic training.

And maybe Jace wouldn't have.

He had, according to one of his many caseworkers, "authority issues."

At the time, Jace wasn't sure he had anything of value to offer to his country, let alone a girl like Sarah. Under the circumstances, leaving seemed like the right thing to do.

Even if saying goodbye had left him feeling as decimated as the pieces of wooden fencing scattered on the ground.

The border collie intercepted Jace a few yards from the ATV. He reached down to give the dog's velvety ears a scratch.

Sarah barely glanced his way. She was busy unhooking the bungee cords wrapped around a chain saw on the back of the ATV.

Did she plan on moving the tree herself?

Jace started to reach for it. "Let me do that."

Her head snapped up. "I can operate a chain saw."

Jace had no doubt she could. But she didn't *have* to. Not while he was here.

He smiled. "I know it's not an axe, but I won't cut myself. Promise."

Sarah didn't return the smile. Her lips compressed even more, as if she was trying to control her response.

And he knew why. Jace hadn't been in a position to make any promises that summer.

Another wave of regret washed over him. He'd been a mixed-up, angry kid back then, and in trying to do good, he'd ended up treating Sarah badly. At the time, a clean break seemed like the best way to end things. But maybe it had been the best for him.

Jace was afraid if they stayed in touch, it would be impossible to keep his emotions in check. Jace was a realist, not a dreamer, nor did he think that good things could last. He'd let enough people down. He didn't want to add Sarah to the list.

"I'll help you haul branches, Mom."

Jace's gaze lit on Addie.

And there was the proof he'd done the right thing.

It shouldn't have surprised Jace that Sarah had married. Started a family.

What surprised Jace was the way his gut clenched at the thought.

Dustin Mueller, Sarah's on-again, off-again boyfriend, had been better for her anyway. Jace had no doubt Crosse Creek's golden boy and future partner at his daddy's law firm had stepped in to take Jace's place. But where was the guy now? Because it sure didn't look like he was involved with the camp.

Jace's gaze shifted to Sarah's left hand, but she was wearing work gloves.

Sarah turned toward her daughter. Her lips softened in a smile that didn't include Jace. "I appreciate that, sweetheart, but what I need you to do is saddle up Star and make sure the west trail is open. I have to get back to the archery range and set up the targets this week."

"Okay!" Addie didn't have to be asked twice. She tossed a smile over her shoulder as she bounded away. "Bye, Mr. Jace! I'll see you later!"

He held out his hand, held his breath.

Sarah finally handed over the chain saw, but something in her eyes told Jace that was all she would let him do.

He was also pretty sure he wouldn't be seeing Addie again.

"What's up, Mom?" Addie bounded into the kitchen, a spring in her step, but Sarah wasn't fooled. Her expression reminded Sarah a little of Maisey whenever she got caught chewing the squeaker out of a new toy.

Between cutting up the tree and fixing the fence, Sarah hadn't had a chance to talk to her daughter since she'd discovered the downed tree that morning.

Sarah set her phone down and motioned Addie into the kitchen, the voicemail from Countryside Caterers playing on repeat in her mind. According to Trish, the owner, they couldn't spare an employee for the summer but would be happy to provide meals for the campers—at a price that came close to Four Arrows' annual fuel bill.

Time for plan B. Except she didn't have one. Or a plan C, either, for that matter.

But right now, Sarah had a more pressing issue to deal with.

"I wanted to talk to you about…Jace." Saying his name, seeing him on Maggie's porch. Working side by side with him. It all felt a little surreal.

"Isn't it great he showed up this morning?" Addie's smile came out in full force. "And right when we needed him!"

No. Just…*no*.

Sarah was not going to let Jace Marshall be the hero who came riding in to save the day. He was the man who'd *left* when she'd needed him the most.

But she couldn't tell her daughter that.

"Addie…why didn't you tell me you'd sent out those cards? And how did you know where to send them?"

"I overheard you talking to Mrs. Hoffman and it sounded like you were upset. There was a date on the cards, so I looked up their last names in Miss Maggie's book and used the computer in the school library to find their addresses."

Addie's resourcefulness didn't surprise Sarah.

"What have I always told you? If you're worried about something, you can always come to me."

Addie ducked her chin. "I didn't tell you because I didn't want to get your hopes up."

Oh, Addie.

Her daughter hadn't been worried about something. She'd been worried about Sarah.

And here Sarah thought she'd been hiding her emotions so well. She made a mental note to make sure Addie wasn't within earshot when she was on the phone.

"Those cards were given to Maggie a long time ago," she said gently. "If I need help, I'll reach out to the volunteers."

"But you tried! I saw the list you made and all the names were crossed out."

Mental note number two: don't leave her planner out. It probably wouldn't be a bad idea to hide Maggie's guest book, an enormous tome that held the names of all the previous campers, from junior detectives, either.

"Sweetheart, the camp isn't your responsibility. You take care of Star and leave the rest to me."

Addie's forehead wrinkled. In that instant, she looked so much like Jace that Sarah's breath caught in her throat.

What if he'd noticed, too?

Over the last ten years, there'd been moments Sarah had thought about contacting Jace, but the memory of their last conversation had stopped her from reaching out to him.

"I know long distance relationships can be challenging," Sarah had told Jace. "But we can make it work."

Instead of agreeing, he'd laughed at her.

"Maybe…but we aren't in a relationship." His lip had curled on the last word, as if that, too, was a joke. "This has been fun but I never made any promises, Sarah."

Fun.

Sarah couldn't believe this was the same person who'd told her that he'd never met anyone like her. Held her like he'd never wanted to let go…

She shook the memory away and focused on Addie. "We'll be fine," she said firmly. "And we'll keep praying."

"But God already answered our prayer!"

Sarah tamped down a groan. "It was…nice…that Jace stopped by after he got your card, but he has a life of his own." He could be married, have a family, for all Sarah knew. "He left town hours ago and—"

"No, he didn't!"

Ordinarily, Sarah would have gently reprimanded her daughter for interrupting, but at the moment, she was too shocked. "What do you mean?"

Jace had spent the morning cutting up the tree while Sarah repaired the fence. After they'd finished, she'd thanked him politely and finally started to breathe again when he'd gotten back into his truck and driven away.

"He was fixing Maggie's steps when I checked on Star after dinner."

Fixing...

Sarah was already rising to her feet. "I'll be back in a few minutes."

"Can I come with you?"

"No." Sarah saw Addie flinch and realized the word had come out more forcefully than she'd intended. "Jace and I—" Once upon a time, those three words had been at the heart of Sarah's future dreams. But once upon a time only happened in fairy tales. Now it felt like her past had come back to haunt her. "—have some things to discuss."

Like why he'd returned after Sarah had made it clear she had everything under control.

She grabbed her jacket and fisted her shaking hands in the pockets.

The sun had started to slip below the trees but a light she hadn't remembered leaving on glowed in the windows of the lodge.

Sarah distinctly remembered locking the front door, though, which meant Jace was trespassing.

The steps didn't shift under her weight this time and the faint smell of fresh cedar seasoned the air. Jace hadn't fixed the weathered boards—he'd replaced them.

Sarah paused at the top, mentally rehearsing what she was going to say, but the door swung open before she could knock, almost as if Jace had been expecting her.

Chapter Three

He'd been expecting her.

Jace stepped to the side and Sarah swept past him without a word, leaving the subtle but unmistakable scent of lilacs in her wake.

He remembered that, too.

It was a little terrifying, really, how much Jace remembered.

"How did you get in here?" Sarah stopped in the center of the gathering room, her gaze skimming over the windows, almost as if she were expecting to see broken glass.

Jace tried not to wince. He probably deserved that.

"Maggie showed me where she kept the spare key."

Would Sarah notice the remnants of the food he'd picked up at the grocery store deli during his brief foray into Crosse Creek?

She did. Whirled to face him again.

"What—"

"It's a pizza."

His attempt to lighten the moment backfired. Jace motioned to the lumpy, threadbare couch that sagged in the middle like an underbaked cake. Maggie had been more about comfort than style, and with dozens of rowdy campers traipsing in and out of the lodge, she'd put her time and energy into making their experience memorable rather than updating the decor. "Maybe we should sit down."

And now Sarah spotted his duffel bag.

"You can't be here."

Jace would have understood her anger. He knew he deserved that, too. It was the panic in Sarah's green eyes that caught him off guard.

"Maggie invited me," Jace said evenly. "The letter I mentioned this morning? She said if I ever needed a place to stay again, I was always welcome here." No matter what had—or hadn't—happened between him and Sarah, Jace should have responded when Maggie had reached out to him the first time. "You and I both know she meant it."

Sarah's throat worked but she couldn't deny it. Maggie's hospitality, her generosity, were as genuine as her smile.

"I already told you that I don't need any help," she said tightly.

"But Four Arrows does." Jace wasn't going to list all the things in need of repair that he'd noticed around the property. "And I gave that card to *Maggie*. Made a promise to her that I intend to keep."

Because he owed Maggie. And whether Sarah liked it or not, Jace owed her something, too.

"I'm free for the next two weeks," Jace went on. "Give me a list and I'll have things in shape for the camp's opening."

"You can't just…swoop in and take over… And why are you smiling?" Anger flared in her expressive green eyes. But she was still beautiful. Still Sarah. Still the girl who, in spite of his best efforts, had been impossible to forget.

"I enlisted in the army ten years ago." Jace should have doused the smile but felt it expand instead. "And I'm a helicopter pilot, so the swooping in thing…it's kind of what I do."

Two. Weeks.

Funny how two little words had the power to keep her awake all night.

Sarah stared up at her bedroom ceiling. At least if she'd fallen asleep, it would have been easier to convince herself that Jace's arrival and their last conversation—when he'd informed her that he was staying—was only a dream.

Having Jace on the property was challenging enough, but how was she supposed to keep Jace and Addie apart when her daughter was convinced that Jace was an answer to her prayers?

Firewood, that's how.

Replenishing what they'd burned last season would keep him busy for days.

Campfire had been a nightly tradition during the summer for all the campers. Singing. Storytelling. S'mores. Maggie had understood that friendships and faith were forged and strengthened in the circle around a crackling fire.

It was where Sarah had seen Jace for the first time.

Memories she'd locked away found a chink in Sarah's internal armor and rushed in.

She'd joined Maggie's team of volunteers and driven the five miles from Crosse Creek to Four Arrows several days a week every summer since her freshman year of high school.

Sarah had loved working in the stables. Loved the quiet trails that wound through the woods and getting to know the horses and their personalities.

After graduation, Sarah's father had wanted her to work at the clinic's reception desk, but one of the wranglers who'd supervised the equestrian camps had accepted a last-minute job offer from a state park. Maggie had asked Sarah if she was interested in taking the woman's place.

Not only had Sarah been interested, she'd been ecstatic.

Her father hadn't approved, of course, but Sarah had managed to convince him that working for a non-profit would look good on a résumé, too. She'd learned at an early age that when it came to Dr. Franklin Crosse, reputation was everything.

Ordinarily, Sarah's day ended when the dinner bell rang, but her hours had changed along with her duties, so she'd stayed for Campfire to familiarize herself with the names and faces of the girls who'd signed up for the overnight trail rides.

That's when she'd noticed the lean, dark-eyed boy standing just outside the circle, his lips twisted in a parody of a smile as one of the counselors strummed the opening notes of a popular worship song on his guitar.

Two other strangers had flanked him—a tall boy in a wrinkled button-down and khakis, and a slender girl wearing a sleeveless dress and a chunky necklace the same shade of turquoise blue as her long, corkscrew curls.

Maggie had had a rule that both the counselors and volunteers wear T-shirts with the Four Arrows logo for easy identification, so Sarah didn't know what their role could be at the camp. They all looked close to Sarah's age, but different enough in appearance that she doubted they were siblings.

She'd tried to concentrate on the music but for some reason, Sarah's gaze had kept shifting to the newcomer in the center of the trio.

Until she had caught him staring back.

Mortified, Sarah had trained her attention on the worship leader, but when it was time to distribute the ingredients for the s'mores, it had been impossible to avoid him.

Khaki Boy had stuttered a thank-you as he and the girl with the mermaid hair both accepted a chocolate bar, but their companion had looked at Sarah almost disdainfully.

"Thanks, but I'll pass."

"You don't like s'mores?" Sarah didn't know why she'd pushed. Maybe because while everyone else had been singing, she'd caught him looking up at the stars like he'd never seen them before.

"Things that are too sweet make me nauseous," he'd drawled.

It had taken Sarah a moment—and a chuckle from Mermaid Girl—to realize the barb was meant for her.

But Sarah hadn't spent the last four summers watching Maggie Malone handle situations with humor and grace without picking up some skills of her own.

In this particular case, Sarah had chosen humor.

"Maggie wants everyone at Four Arrows to be healthy, so I'll be sure to tell Mrs. Hoffman, the camp cook, that you're skipping dessert while you're here," she'd told him.

The other boy had stifled a laugh.

Sarah had bravely met his friend's gaze again but this time, she saw a spark of something that wasn't disdain. Curiosity? Approval?

Either way, it had rattled Sarah. Her knees and her heart had felt a little shaky when she'd moved away. Which Sarah found a little disturbing, because she'd dated Dustin Mueller on and off since their sophomore year and he'd never had that effect on her.

The next day, the boy had shown up at the stable with Maggie.

"Sarah… I'd like you to meet Jace Marshall. He's going to be staying here for a while. I was going to give him a tour of the camp, but my signature is required for a delivery, so I was hoping you'd have time to fill in for me."

Staying here.

Sarah's heart had snagged on the words. He wasn't with the church group renting the camp for the next two weeks. Nor— Sarah *may* have checked—was his name on the roster of new volunteers.

Which meant… Jace Marshall was a bit of a mystery.

But she couldn't say no to Maggie's request, so that left her playing tour guide.

Jace hadn't looked happy with the arrangement, either.

Autumn had stretched her neck over the stall but instead of recoiling—kind of like Jace had done when he'd walked into the stable and spotted Sarah organizing the tack box—he'd patted the mare's velvety nose.

"Do you ride?" she'd asked briskly, determined to treat him like any other guest.

"Not many horses where I live."

Sarah had wanted to ask where that was, but the tense line of Jace's shoulders hinted that he wasn't comfortable with small talk. Or maybe he just didn't like talking to her.

"We'll cover more ground and get this over faster on horseback."

"I'll give it a try," Jace had said, so swiftly that it made Sarah grin when she should have been offended.

For a split second, he'd looked shocked. And then he'd flashed a grin back at her. "I suppose you're going to give me the one that bucks and kicks."

Actually, Sarah was going to saddle up the perfect fit for a novice rider. She clicked her tongue and heard a shuffling sound in the depths of the stall, followed by a dry cough.

She had unlatched the door and slid it open. The paint horse nickered softly when Sarah ran her hand down its withers. She'd tossed a look over her shoulder at Jace.

"I think you can handle this one. He only has one gear."

She'd given Jace a quick tutorial so he ended up in the saddle and not the ground. They rode to the waterfront and the archery range and Sarah pointed out the building where the campers did arts and crafts. She had cut through the field where some of the counselors were setting up an obstacle course before looping back to the barn.

Jace hadn't said a word the entire time they were together, so Sarah didn't learn anything about him. Where he was from or why he was there.

That information had come later. From, of all people, Sarah's father.

"I heard that one of the camp donors convinced Maggie to take in three foster kids for the summer," he'd told her at breakfast the next morning, the edge in his tone conveying his thoughts on the matter. "I tell you, Maggie Malone has more good intentions than common sense sometimes, taking on a lost cause."

Sarah had wanted to defend Maggie but it wouldn't have mattered. Once her father had formed an opinion, it never changed. She knew Maggie's heart for people. And even though Sarah had just met Jace Marshall, something told her that he wasn't a lost cause. And she'd been right.

The memories faded and pride welled up inside of Sarah.

Jace had joined the military. Was a pilot.

She'd always seen his potential—even when Jace hadn't seen it in himself.

Her father wouldn't have understood, so Sarah was careful not to talk about Jace. Just like she didn't talk about her mother, who'd abandoned them when Sarah was only five years old. But as it turned out she didn't have to. A volunteer from Crosse Creek Community had mentioned seeing Sarah laughing with "a boy" at the camp and he'd confronted her.

Sarah had taken a chance and told her father that she and Jace had become friends. He'd been livid instead of understanding.

"Don't get involved with him, Sarah. A boy like that will break your heart."

As it turned out, her father had been right.

Wednesday. Day two of Jace's Banishment to the Forest.

Sure, *firewood* had been the only thing written on the piece of paper he'd found taped to the door the morning after he'd told Sarah he was staying, but Jace knew better. Locating downed trees, cutting them up and loading them into the back of his truck for transport to the lean-to by the firepit separated him from the main camp. And everyone who lived there.

Jace wasn't sure why that bothered him so much.

This was an op. Get in and get out. The "swooping in" Sarah had accused Jace of doing. He couldn't help the way God had hardwired him, though. Precision and absolute focus on the mission in front of him were the reasons his call sign was Falcon.

Except…the past kept messing with his head.

Oh, who was he kidding?

Not only the past, but a green-eyed woman who clearly didn't want him around.

He'd occasionally caught a glimpse of Sarah dropping hay bales off in the round pen or washing windows on the cabins. He'd see lights glowing in the barn before dawn and long after sunset, proof she was working too hard.

But why was she working *here*? Living here? Alone, except for her daughter?

A hundred questions ricocheted around Jace's head, but the only person who could answer them was doing her best to avoid him.

Well, Sarah couldn't avoid him anymore. Jace had split and stacked enough firewood to take Campfire through this summer and into the next. He'd report—in person—for his next assignment as soon as he'd changed clothes and reheated the container of chicken soup that had appeared on the doorstep of the lodge along with the note.

More than likely, Sarah hadn't wanted Jace to starve to death before he completed the task he'd been given, but still. It meant she was thinking about him.

Only fair, because Jace couldn't stop thinking about *her*.

He stripped off his work gloves and dropped them on the bench in the laundry room tucked behind Maggie's office. Paused to flex out the knot that had settled in his shoulder. But the price of running a chain saw for eight hours and spending time in the woods was worth a few aches and pains.

He'd forgotten how beautiful it was here. A hundred acres of mature hardwood and pine, a perfect setting for the lake embedded like a sapphire in the center of the property.

Jace had hated it at first.

He hadn't appreciated the silence. Sunrises a vibrant wash of orange and crimson. The sharp scent of pine. Stars that made him feel even more insignificant than he already did.

Until he'd seen it through Sarah's eyes.

And there he went. Thinking about her again.

Jace set thoughts of Sarah firmly to the side. He continued down the narrow hallway and stopped when he reached the small, paneled room at the back of the lodge that served as the camp's infirmary.

He'd done a little recon the day he'd arrived. Maggie's second-floor apartment was still furnished, but Jace didn't feel right about staying there. The infirmary had a cot and a window— pretty decent digs compared to where he'd been stationed the last eighteen months. And he'd be gone before the camp opened for the season, freeing up the space again.

He switched out his sawdust-encrusted clothes for a clean T-shirt and jeans before padding up the stairs. Out of necessity, Jace did need to eat, and Maggie's private living quarters included a separate kitchenette—convenient for those rare times she didn't join the campers in the dining hall. There was a microwave, a two-burner range, a sink and a dorm-sized refrigerator.

And a loaf of banana bread on the counter.

Jace's mouth watered just looking at it. Soup had become the second course.

He warmed both up in the microwave and lowered himself onto one of the wooden chairs by the window. It was quiet. The good kind that settled a guy's soul, instead of making him feel restless. Through the trees, a sudden flash of light illuminated the barn and Jace frowned.

It was almost nine o'clock.

Sarah took really good care of the horses but did she have to read them a story and tuck them into bed at night, too?

Jace tossed back the last piece of bread and rose to his feet.

Now that he had a lock on Sarah's location, this might be a good time to ask for his next assignment.

And apologize.

Because that was something God had been nudging Jace to do.

Even if Sarah rejected it, the way she'd tried to reject his help.

He crossed the yard to the stable and slid open the door, his heart thumping like the props of his helo.

"Hi!"

Jace pulled up short at the cheerful greeting.

Sarah's daughter, Addie, sat cross-legged in a cotton candy–pink folding chair blocking the center aisle between the stalls, a book balanced in her lap and a bowl of popcorn on the floor beside her.

Sarah was nowhere in sight, but Addie hopped to her feet as Jace started to back up.

"Are you looking for my mom? She fell asleep while we were watching *Anne of Green Gables*. It's my favorite… Have you ever seen it?"

That would be a negative.

Jace shook his head.

"Anne has red hair, like me." Addie tugged on the end of her copper ponytail. "She likes to read, too."

"Mmm."

As an only child who'd chosen a career in the military, Jace hadn't been around kids very often. He didn't know what to say, but Addie didn't seem to mind doing all the talking. And she was good at it.

In less than ten minutes, Jace was given an overview of the characters and the plot. By the time Addie finished, his head was spinning.

"That sounds…interesting," he murmured.

"Maybe you can watch it with us sometime!" Addie's brown eyes sparkled.

A loud thump from behind one of the stall doors prevented Jace from having to respond.

Addie jumped up and followed the sound to its source. She rose up on her tiptoes and peered inside the stall. "What's the matter?" she crooned. "Were we making too much noise while you were trying to sleep?"

Another distinct thump. The sound of a hoof striking the wall.

Addie unhooked the latch and started to open the door.

"Wait!" Jace covered the short distance between them. Other than the three months he'd spent at Four Arrows, his experience with horses was minimal, but he knew they could be unpredictable.

Addie paused but it was too late. The horse nosed the door open and stepped into the aisle.

"Whoa…" Jace put himself between Addie and the escapee and found himself face-to-face with… "Pancakes?"

The brown and white paint's ears tilted in his direction.

Addie's eyes went wide. "Mom said you stayed here a long time ago. Was Pancakes your horse?"

Jace nodded.

Only because Sarah had a wicked sense of humor.

Pancakes was the most easygoing mount—and the slowest—in the entire herd. Which was why Sarah had saddled him for Jace when Maggie had asked her to take him on a tour of the camp. Payback for Jace being rude at Campfire, but Sarah hadn't known it was self-preservation on his part.

Even before she'd noticed him, Jace had noticed her. Talking with some of the campers. Helping a counselor set up chairs. Totally at ease in her surroundings while Jace felt completely out of his element.

Oh, and she was beautiful, too.

All the college-bound guys who'd signed up to be camp

counselors had been sneaking looks at Sarah, too, which only made Jace more determined not to.

"He remembers you." Addie giggled as Pancakes bumped his head against Jace's shoulder.

Jace was experiencing déjà vu again. It seemed like everywhere he went, he ran straight into a memory. "Or he smells the popcorn."

A shrill whinny from another stall had Addie giggling again. "I think Star is jealous. Do you want to meet her?"

What else could Jace say?

"Sure."

He coaxed a reluctant Pancakes back into the stall and fastened the latch before following Addie down the row of stalls.

She slid open the last door and a coal-black mare stepped into the aisle. Addie flung her arms around the horse's neck and it lipped her hair, proving the affection was mutual.

"Star is her barn name. Her real name is Wish on a Falling Star." Addie rubbed the mare's nose. "My mom named her. The night I was born, she saw a falling star over the lake." Addie traced an invisible arch in the air with her finger. "She was supposed to help Miss Maggie deliver Star, but they had to go to the hospital instead so she could have me. Miss Maggie called me and Star her spring foals because we were born the same night."

Maggie had driven Sarah to the hospital?

An internal alarm sounded in Jace's head, the way it did right before an op went south.

"But what about…" *your dad*, he wanted to say. But what if something bad had happened to Dustin? He didn't want to open the door to a painful memory. "Your grandpa?"

Addie looked confused by the question. "Grandpa Crosse? He wasn't there. He moved away before I was born."

Moved away?

Crosse Creek had been founded by Sarah's relatives. Her

father was a pillar of the tight-knit community. Jace couldn't imagine what would cause Dr. Crosse to leave any more than he could fathom why Sarah had stayed.

"Isn't it kind of cool that Star and I have the same birthday? We can celebrate on the same day."

Jace managed a nod. None of this was making sense.

"Last year, we took the horses to Maple Hill. Did you go there when you stayed at Four Arrows?"

Her shining eyes—*brown* eyes—met Jace's and everything around him disappeared. The music playing in the background. The low nickers from the horses in their stalls.

"Once." Jace's voice hitched on the word.

"It's awesome." Addie patted Star's withers. "I think it's one of the best places God made in the whole world. Mom said it might be too cold to stay overnight, but I told her we could bring extra blankets and I'd help her put up the tent and everything.

"I was supposed to be born in May but I was a whole month early. It was my golden birthday in April so she said okay," she continued without taking a breath. "Ten on the tenth. I'm short for my age, but Maggie said it's the size of your heart that counts."

Ten.

Sarah's daughter was ten.

Jace's throat closed.

That meant...

"Addie?"

The pieces all fell into place as Sarah walked into the barn.

Chapter Four

The floor shifted beneath Sarah's feet when she saw Jace standing next to her daughter.

"Mom, you'll never guess what! Pancakes remembers Mr. Jace from when he stayed at camp!"

What else had they talked about?

A wave of panic washed over her. Sarah stole a glance at Jace, but nothing in his expression revealed his thoughts.

"Addie…" Sarah worked up a smile. "It's past your bedtime."

"But it's summer vacation! Can't I stay up a little later?"

"Dr. Callahan will be stopping over for the horses' spring checkups in a few days, and I'll be trimming hooves and giving baths tomorrow, so if you want to help, you'll need a good night's sleep."

Addie turned to Jace. "I want to be a veterinarian when I grow up," she told him. "That way we can save money and the camp won't—"

"I'll be there in a few minutes," Sarah interrupted.

Jace had already noticed the camp was showing signs of wear and tear. He didn't need to know the state of their bank account, too. "Don't forget to brush your teeth."

"I won't." Addie shooed Star back into the stall and danced back to her chair to grab the bowl of popcorn. "'Night, Mr. Jace. See you in the morning!"

"'Night." His husky voice scraped across Sarah's already sensitive nerves.

The last thing she remembered was Anne Shirley rejecting Gilbert Blythe's apology. She must have drifted off for a few minutes and Addie had taken the opportunity to sneak out of the cabin and spend some time with Star.

The past few days, Sarah had managed to keep Addie occupied, afraid that her natural curiosity would cause her to seek Jace out. It hadn't crossed her mind that it would be the other way around.

Either way, Sarah couldn't live like this.

"I'll be rounding up some volunteers for next week," she said, hating the rattle in her voice. Why did Jace still have such an effect on her? "Once they clean cabins and get the waterfront ready, things will be in pretty good shape. It helped a lot that you replenished the firewood, so there's no reason for you to stay."

"Isn't there?"

It was the strange inflection in Jace's voice—not the question—that had Sarah swallowing hard.

"If you're on leave, I don't want the camp to take up any more of your time."

"When were you going to tell me?"

Sarah frowned. "I just drew up a list of possible volunteers this afternoon."

"Not about that. About…" A muscle worked in Jace's jaw. "Addie. When were you going to tell me that I have a daughter?"

Sarah's heart dropped. She stared at him, not knowing what to say.

"You *weren't*." Jace breathed into the silence. "You were going to let me leave…" His teeth snapped together, as if he was barely holding on to whatever emotion shadowed his eyes.

"You did before, knowing that…you could be a father." Sarah hated that her voice came out low, shaky, but Jace flinched.

"Addie is my child, Sarah. You didn't think I had a right to know?"

"A right?" she echoed. "You're the one who said you didn't

want to be tied down. Addie was a gift…not a burden or an obligation. You left, Jace. And you never called. Never came back. You made a life and so did I. Don't question the decision I made because *you* made one first."

Sarah was surprised at the bitterness that leached into her voice.

At Maggie's urging, Sarah had forgiven him, and yet she couldn't erase the past. Jace Marshall had broken her heart, but Sarah had to protect Addie's. Ten years may have gone by, but that didn't mean he'd changed.

And he proved it when he turned and strode out of the barn.

Jace doubled over, hands braced on his knees, sucking in lungfuls of fresh air.

He'd been trained to handle the unexpected, but retreat had seemed like the wisest course of action.

He needed time for his emotions to settle until he could see straight again. Talk to Sarah instead of demanding answers.

Jace retraced his steps to the lodge on autopilot.

Now the panic in Sarah's eyes the day he'd arrived made sense. No wonder she hadn't wanted him here. When Jace had insisted on staying, she'd put him on firewood duty. Not because she hadn't wanted to see him—because she hadn't wanted him to spend time with Addie and guess the truth.

But Jace, who had a reputation in his unit for being the details guy, had completely missed the clues. Addie's age. Eyes the same shade of brown as his. Because Jace had assumed that Sarah had done exactly what Dr. Crosse claimed she would do after Jace left. Go to med school. Fall in love with someone who deserved her.

The front door snapped shut behind Jace as he strode past the check-in desk, the weight of the memories pressing down on his shoulders.

It's too much, Lord.

He needed some space. Time to recalibrate.

Jace pulled out his duffel bag, grabbed the clothes he'd piled on the chair and began to stuff them inside.

He'd tried to do the right thing. The best thing. He hadn't wanted to cause a wedge between Sarah and her father, but it had happened anyway. He'd left town and Sarah had moved in with Maggie. Given birth to Addie a month early. Raised her on her own.

Jace's breath rattled in his chest.

An image of Addie's sparkling eyes and bright smile flashed in Jace's mind.

What had Sarah told their daughter about him?

Jace knew what it was like to grow up without a dad. Brad Marshall had completely checked out after Jace's mom had died. Not that the guy would have won a Father of the Year award before that. Jace would have been terrified at the thought of becoming a father, but he wouldn't have bailed on Sarah and Addie.

You never called. You never came back. You made a life and so did I...

Sarah's words cycled back and landed like another punch to the gut.

In her mind, he'd abandoned them both.

Jace's chest burned.

If she'd known how many times he'd been tempted to call, just to hear her voice. The dozens of text messages he'd written and then deleted.

Jace had told himself that a clean break was best for both of them, but if he was honest with himself, there'd been the subconscious fear that Sarah would have eventually realized her father was right and rejected him.

After five different foster homes in as many years, Jace had figured out it hurt less if you didn't look back.

Now the last ten years unfolded in his head. All the firsts

he'd missed in Addie's life. First steps. First day of school. Birthdays. Christmases.

Jace had been living his life, oblivious to the fact that his daughter was growing up without a dad.

Maggie should have contacted him. She'd known Sarah was expecting. And as close as the two women were, Sarah would have confided that Jace was the father. Had she asked Maggie to keep her pregnancy a secret? Or, like Dr. Crosse, had Maggie come to the conclusion that Sarah and her child would be better off without him?

In the letter Maggie had written while Jace was at boot camp, she'd told him that she was praying for him and gave him an update on the camp. The only time she'd mentioned Sarah was in reference to a foal that had been born.

Sarah helped Dr. Callahan deliver Autumn's first foal.

Jace sat down hard on the cot.

Because Sarah should have been in college by then, not still at Four Arrows.

Maggie had given Jace a clue and he'd missed it. Then, in the next sentence, she'd extended an invitation.

You're missed, Jace. And you'll always have a home here, if you decide to come back.

Jace had never responded. Maggie hadn't reached out again and now he wondered if ignoring her letter had confirmed that he didn't deserve someone like Sarah.

And maybe that hadn't changed.

The fact that Sarah hadn't planned to tell Jace that he was a father was another clue. Evidence she didn't *want* him in Addie's life. Or hers.

Jace's lips twisted.

If that was Sarah's wish, he could make it come true.

Addie had declared he was an answer to prayer, but Sarah sure didn't see it that way.

Jace grabbed his jacket and a yellow rock fell off the chair and spun across the floor.

The rock he'd found half buried in the leaves on the North Path. He picked it up, only this time the word painted on the surface seemed like it had been meant for him.

TRUST.

The verse Maggie had written in the front cover of the Bible she'd stashed in Jace's suitcase swept through his mind and he closed his eyes.

Trust in the Lord with all thine heart, and lean not unto thine own understanding. In all thy ways acknowledge Him, and He shall direct thy paths.

Jace had spent the first eighteen years of his life stumbling blindly along, trying to figure out where he was going. What he was supposed to do. Who he was supposed to be. Until he'd reached out to God and found his way again.

And trust is what it came down to now.

Addie might have sent the original missive asking Jace to come back to Four Arrows, but God had been at work, too. Jace had almost skipped the quick layover at his apartment and gone straight to Mason's place. If he had, he wouldn't have seen Addie's card.

Jace turned the rock over in his hands before setting it on the table beside the cot.

He couldn't make up for the years he'd lost with Addie, but he was here now.

And no matter how Sarah felt about Jace, like it or not, she needed him.

The next morning, Sarah shuffled over to the coffee pot to find out if a second helping of caffeine would dispel the fog in her head.

She'd just lifted the mug to take a sip when a soft knock on the door of the cabin broke the silence. Through the curtain, she could see a tall, broad-shouldered shape.

The coffee burned a path down Sarah's throat.

Why was he still here? The promise he'd made to Maggie? Because his whispered promises to Sarah had lasted as long as the morning mist over the lake.

Jace wasn't the kind of man she could rely on.

After his abrupt departure from the barn, Sarah had expected him to pack up his things and be long gone before the sun came up.

Hoped, honestly, because it would have been easier than facing him now that he knew the truth.

Sarah glanced at Addie's bedroom door. Still closed. Somehow, Sarah had managed to watch the rest of the movie with Addie after she'd returned to the cabin and pretend that everything was fine. Something she'd perfected over the years, although Maggie had seen through Sarah's attempt to hide her scars.

Another knock.

She considered ignoring it, but this one was a little louder and propelled Sarah toward the door.

She pulled in a breath and opened it, knowing Jace would see the evidence of another sleepless night in her bloodshot eyes. At least she was dressed, although the sweatpants and faded T-shirt she'd fallen asleep in looked a little rumpled from tossing and turning all night.

"Sarah." Unlike her, Jace looked rested and ready to start the day. Clear-eyed and steady, even though he'd looked completely wrecked the night before.

Sarah slipped outside. Wrapped her arms around her middle. Addie might be asleep at the moment, but it wouldn't be long before she jumped out of bed to say good morning to Star.

"I thought you left." Sarah kept her voice low, but it still sounded like an accusation.

"I'm sorry. I shouldn't have walked out like that...but I needed some time to...regroup...and I thought you might, too."

Sarah hadn't expected an apology. And she *had* needed time to regroup.

What she didn't need, on top of cancellations and staffing issues and a never-ending to-do list, was Jace's magnetic pull on the heart he'd casually broken.

It had occurred to Sarah that now that he'd had time to "regroup," he could demand a paternity test. Or inform Sarah that he planned to hire an attorney and take her to court if she refused to let him spend time with Addie. He'd abandoned them, but it didn't change the fact that he was Addie's father. And fathers had rights.

Sarah swallowed hard. "What do you want, Jace?"

"The next item on the to-do list."

Sarah stared at him.

"You...you don't want Addie to know you're her father?"

A shadow passed through Jace's eyes.

"Of course I want her to know," he said quietly. "But you're her mother. You know her better than anyone else, so you get to decide when that happens."

"Whatcha doing?"

Jace's head jerked up at the sound of Addie's lilting voice. He hadn't seen her since the night she'd introduced him to Star—and he had found out that she was his daughter.

By design, no doubt.

Sarah was being protective and Jace had to be patient even though he wanted to spend time with Addie.

And Sarah.

Jace found himself watching for a glimpse of them during the day. Resisting the urge to seek them out in the evening when he saw lights glowing through the windows of their cabin.

When Sarah had asked Jace what he wanted, he'd seen the

fear in her eyes. Until that moment, he hadn't known the answer. But when it had came to him, if he'd dared to say it out loud, Sarah would have slammed the door in his face for sure. She still didn't trust him.

Why would she? Everything she'd accused him of was true. Except the real reason he'd left.

Jace wanted to do more than knock off an item on the camp's to-do list, but that inner nudge kept reminding him to wait.

"I just took off the snowplow and now I'm putting on the mower deck." He answered Addie's question, rolled back on the balls of his feet and surveyed his work.

He'd finished his last task earlier than expected and looked for something else to do. Unfortunately, it hadn't taken long. The more Jace explored the camp, the more items he added to his own to-do list.

"Mom doesn't do that until the Fourth of July…just in case we get more snow," Addie said.

"You're kidding."

Addie grinned. "Uh-huh."

Jace found himself grinning back.

Once upon a time, Sarah had teased him, too. Nicknamed him Mr. Serious. She'd been more like Addie that summer. Bubbly and sweet. In retaliation, Jace had dubbed her Miss Blue Skies and Sunshine.

Running the camp was a 24/7 job, and so was being a parent. Sarah was doing both alone and now she was the serious one.

Jace wondered if he was to blame for that, too.

"But we do get snow in May sometimes." Addie plopped down next to Jace. "We had an ice storm right before school got out and there was no electricity. Mom and I stayed in the lodge for a few days because our cabin doesn't have a generator.

"Then the ceiling started to leak and Mom had to go up in the attic. That's when she found the box with Maggie's wishing cards." Addie tipped her head. "Mom said you spent the whole summer here because you didn't have anywhere else to go."

Jace nodded.

That was true, although Sarah had softened the edges of the story.

Jace had turned eighteen two weeks before graduation, and the Wainrights had called him into their living room and informed him that after the ceremony, he would need to make other "living arrangements."

Jace didn't blame them. Rob and Sandy Wainright were decent people but they were also foster family number five. Jace had been placed with them at the start of the school year and rebuffed all their attempts to make him feel at home. He'd told them so many times that he wanted to be left alone that they'd finally taken him seriously. Jace's attitude, combined with frequent calls from the school guidance office about his skipping classes, may have factored into their decision, too.

Jace had thanked them, packed up his belongings and left that night. No sense sticking around and waiting for the inevitable.

Jace had worked part-time for a mechanic and knew where he hid the spare key to the shop. For several nights, Jace had sneaked in and slept in the break room until someone saw a light on and called his boss. Instead of calling the police, his boss had called his pastor. The guy had already asked Maggie if she would take in two other foster kids for the summer, so he'd asked Jace if he'd be willing to go, too. Jace wasn't willing. But he was interested in having a roof over his head that wasn't the county jail, so he'd agreed.

"Did you like it here?" Addie picked some blades of grass and began braiding them together.

"I liked the quiet." *I liked your mom.*

He still liked her mom.

Addie tipped her face toward the sun. "I love living here. Mom grew up in Crosse Creek, but she couldn't stay in the house after my grandpa left so Maggie let her move into the cabin. That was before I was born, but I'm glad she picked the one closest to the barn."

Jace had seen Sarah's childhood home. Maggie had asked him to run an errand for her in town and he hadn't been able to resist the urge to drive around, looking for Sarah's address.

Even a town the size of Crosse Creek had a neighborhood made up of stately old homes with manicured lawns, flower beds and mature trees that formed hedges around each house for privacy.

Everything inside of Jace had told him to turn around, but he had kept driving until he reached the end of the cul-de-sac, where the name *Crosse* was engraved on a plaque in the center of one of the stone pillars that flanked the driveway. The brick home was three stories high, with dormers that reminded Jace of turrets.

He'd heard Sarah was the daughter of a doctor, but no one had mentioned that she lived in a castle.

Any illusions Jace might have had about Sarah's father accepting him had vanished. He didn't have roots that went deep into the community. Jace had had a half dozen placements since he'd gone into foster care, but couldn't call a single one of them home. His juvenile file was sealed so Dr. Crosse didn't know he'd been picked up once for vandalism, but Jace couldn't erase the stain on his conscience.

Yeah. A guy with no pedigree, no family, no direction, wouldn't have made the cut with Dr. Crosse.

Addie suddenly bounced to her feet. "I'm going to take Star out for a ride."

Alone?

Was that allowed?

"Where's your mom?" he asked casually.

"She's on the phone with someone." Addie's voice dropped

a notch. "I think it's the bank again. She always sends me out-side when she talks to people at the bank."

Out of the mouths of babes. Isn't that how the saying went?

Was the camp in financial trouble, too?

And who did Sarah confide in, lean on, now that Maggie was gone?

He'd been at the camp for almost a week, and the only other person Jace had seen was a delivery driver. Didn't Sarah have friends? Or did running the camp take up every spare second of her time?

"Do you go riding by yourself a lot?" he asked.

"I'm not alone. I'm with Star," Addie pointed out. "She counts."

Jace wasn't so sure.

He was probably going to get into big trouble with Sarah, but he didn't feel comfortable with Addie venturing off into the woods by herself on horseback.

"If you wait a few minutes while I put the tools away, I can go with you," Jace heard himself say.

Addie's face lit up. "Really? I'll saddle Pancakes! If you haven't ridden in a while, he's bombproof."

Jace thought about the last time he'd maneuvered the helo around a real bomb that had detonated during a patrol. He could handle something with a few more gears.

"Um…maybe one that won't doze off on the trail?" Jace suggested.

And then he saw the mischievous gleam in Addie's eyes.

"You're joking again, aren't you?"

Like mother, like daughter.

Addie's giggle burrowed into Jace's heart and settled there.

He'd promised Sarah he would wait on her timing, but it was going to be harder than he thought. Because Jace wanted to tell the whole world that Addie was his daughter.

Chapter Five

"Thank you for letting me know, Gloria. I understand that things come up."

Sarah resisted the urge to bang the cell phone against her forehead as she ended the call.

One of the groups who'd booked the camp in August had just backed out, leaving her with six empty cabins and another gaping hole in the budget. The nonrefundable deposit wouldn't begin to cover the lost revenue for those two weeks, either.

She could put the word out to some of the church groups that had stayed there in the past, but as the season came to an end, camp attendance naturally declined as people's attention shifted from summer activities to the new school year.

Maybe it was time to face another hard truth.

Camp attendance had been slowly declining anyway. Summer sports camps, family vacations, destinations that offered upscale accommodations over rustic but charming nostalgia. The overnight equine camps that Sarah had started organizing after Maggie's death were popular, but the care and keeping of the small herd during the winter months also happened to be the largest drain on the camp's already-strained budget...

And she wasn't going there. Not yet.

Sarah opened the door and almost tripped over Maisey. The border collie was lying belly-up on the open porch, eyes at half-mast.

"You're supposed to be with Addie, not taking a nap," Sarah scolded.

Maisey's ears twitched before she drifted off to sleep again.

Sarah headed toward the barn. At least when Addie went missing, Sarah knew where to find her.

Guilt added weight to the burden she was already carrying.

Sarah had shooed Addie outside when she'd seen Gloria's name pop up on her caller ID. Gloria's cheerleading squad returned every year, convening at the camp for some fun and team-building exercises before school started, but Sarah had a hunch the coach wouldn't be calling two months before their scheduled arrival just to say hello.

Lord…

The prayer started and stopped, tangled in Sarah's sigh, but it was all she could muster at the moment.

Maggie would have viewed this situation as an opportunity to see God move, but all Sarah could see was another obstacle in her path.

Why couldn't she have faith like Maggie?

Her friend had made trusting God look as easy as breathing.

There'd been a time when it had come naturally to Sarah, too. But after Maggie's death and three years of feeling the weight of all the responsibilities pressing down on her, it was a daily effort to pause and simply remind herself to breathe.

"Addie?" Sarah slid the door open. The horses were turned out during the day, but it wasn't unusual to find Addie in the barn, brushing Star or weaving intricate braids in the horse's mane and tail.

She made her way to the tack room. Addie had been begging her to go on a trail ride the past few days, but Sarah had put her off. She had a million things to do before the camp opened for the season.

Hiding from Jace was now one of them.

Their last conversation had filled Sarah with relief. And doubt.

Jace, not making any demands on her or Addie. Claiming that all he wanted was his next assigned task. She couldn't believe it...

Sarah froze in the doorway of the tack room. The bridles hung like Christmas stockings on hooks along the wall, but Star's was missing. And there was another empty hook right beside it, where Thor's should have been.

Had Jace gone riding with her?

Sarah's pulse stuttered.

The three-year-old gelding was a sweetheart, but he'd just been saddle-broken the previous summer. Sarah exercised all the horses on a regular basis to keep them in shape, but she hadn't had an opportunity to take Thor out on the trails yet. Even the most easygoing horses could be a little hard to handle when they were finally allowed to stretch their legs after a long winter.

Concern about Jace's riding ability threatened to override her frustration that he hadn't kept his word.

Sarah stepped outside and whistled for Autumn. The mare never ventured very far away, content to stay closer to the barn in case Sarah showed up with a treat.

A few seconds later, Autumn trotted out of the woods, ears lifted in anticipation.

"Sorry, girl, not right now," Sarah murmured. She swung onto the red roan's back, not bothering with a saddle or bridle. Unlike a certain someone, Autumn could be trusted.

The trailhead behind the barn separated into four paths and Sarah chose Addie's favorite. The South path cut through an old orchard, planted long before Maggie's grandparents had bought the land. In the spring, apple blossoms bloomed on the branches and Addie loved to linger there. She'd even dubbed it *The Avenue* in honor of Anne Shirley.

As Autumn neared the orchard, the only conversation Sarah could hear was the one between the chickadees and a red squirrel that chattered a warning from its perch on a low branch.

She sat back, cueing the mare to stop, and felt a prickle of unease as she scanned the area.

Addie knew where she was allowed to go and which areas were off-limits unless they were together.

The wooden bridge that linked the North and South paths fell into the second category. For most of the year, the creek that meandered gently through the property was serene and postcard-pretty. This time of year, pumped up by melting snow and spring rains, it sported a bit of an attitude.

"Addie knows not to cross the bridge alone," Sarah told Autumn, patting the horse's neck as if she were the one in need of comfort.

Except… Addie wasn't alone, and Jace wouldn't know that fixing the bridge was one of the things on Sarah's list.

The familiar jingle of reins triggered a rush of relief that was short-lived because the sound had come from behind her, not the orchard.

She twisted in the saddle and saw Star emerge from the woods.

Without a rider.

Sarah's next breath got stuck in her lungs.

Autumn, sensing her distress, didn't wait for a command. She spun around and trotted toward her stablemate.

Sarah slid off Autumn's back, surprised that her knees held her upright, and caught the reins dragging on the ground before they tangled around Star's hooves.

"Easy, girl," she crooned.

Star's nostrils flared but she didn't appear injured or upset. The mare nickered at Autumn before bumping her nose against Sarah's pocket in search of a treat.

"Addie?" Sarah's voice thinned, exposing the fear that coursed through her body.

"I'm right here!" Addie emerged on foot through a break in the trees, breathless but smiling. Oblivious to the fact that she'd taken ten years off her mother's life.

"Are you all right?" Sarah performed a quick scan from the top of Addie's head to the scuffed tips of her cowboy boots.

"Sure." Her daughter looked confused by the question. "I was showing Jace the lightning tree."

In her panic, Sarah had forgotten about another one of Addie's favorite landmarks on the property. The massive oak, one of the oldest on the property, had been struck by lightning several years ago. The top branches were missing and half the trunk bore the mark of the flames, a charred gash that resembled a scar.

"But he wouldn't let me climb it," Addie continued. "Even when I told him I've done it a bazillion times."

"I think your exact word was *gazillion,* but that still wasn't enough to convince me."

The topic of their conversation emerged from the woods. Sarah's gaze shifted to Jace, who looked so comfortable on Thor's back he could have been relaxing in his favorite recliner.

Comfortable and way too attractive in his faded jeans, black T-shirt and hiking boots.

Sarah tore her gaze away and focused on Addie. She had things to say to both of them, but the conversation with Jace could wait until they were alone. "You weren't keeping a very close eye on Star."

Addie heard the gentle reprimand in Sarah's voice and bit her lip. "I'm sorry! I ground tied her, but she must have heard Autumn and wanted to say hi."

Sarah handed her the reins. "We have to get back to the house. I have some phone calls to make." Now she had three slots to fill if there was any hope of staying out of the red.

"But Jace hasn't seen the chapel yet!" Addie protested. "He said it was just an old, run-down cabin the last time he was here."

It was also the place he'd told Sarah there was no room in his life for her.

Tucked in a stand of paper birch, the original homestead was located on one of the most beautiful areas of the property. The cabin had become a meeting place for her and Jace that summer. He'd sent Sarah a text, asking her to meet him there before he left. Sarah had imagined they would make plans for the future but instead, Jace had coolly informed Sarah that he hadn't made any promises.

Sarah had been relieved when a group of volunteers had, at Maggie's request, torn the cabin down a few months after Addie was born. The stone foundation was starting to crumble and Maggie was afraid it would cave in. In its place, a small chapel had been built to use as a private retreat or hold worship services during the weeklong horse camps.

Sarah had watched a group of men raze the rickety structure and haul away the weathered wood. She'd pitched in and helped the volunteer crew paint the walls. With the cabin gone, it was easier for Sarah to stop there with a group of campers and not relive her last conversation with Jace Marshall.

He'd broken her heart when he'd left, but, like the chapel, Sarah had slowly built a new life for her and Addie, one day at a time.

"I can see it later." Jace spoke up before Sarah. "I have a few more things to do this afternoon, too."

Addie nodded, her disappointment evident in the slump of her shoulders as she put one foot in the stirrup and vaulted gracefully onto Star's back.

"But you can come over for supper tonight, right?" Her face brightened. "Mom and I are making homemade pizza and you can pick whatever you want to put on it. We've got pepperoni and sausage. Black olives. Mushrooms." Her pert nose wrinkled. "Mom likes those but I don't. Peppers. Onions…"

Sarah had stopped listening. Because Addie had invited Jace to their cabin. For supper.

Saturday night pizza had been Sarah's idea. Making dinner together, just the two of them, had been a connecting point, a chance for them to spend time together during the busy summer months. But it had been so much fun, they'd decided to continue the tradition throughout the year.

Sarah thought of their tiny cabin, the table with only two chairs, and imagined Jace filling up the entire space when he was already taking up way too much space in her head.

"I'm afraid I already have plans for this evening," Jace was saying. "But thank you for the invitation."

What other plans did Jace have? And why did Sarah feel the tiniest twinge of disappointment?

Oh, no you don't, she told her heart sternly. *We're not doing that again.*

Hadn't Jace just proven he couldn't be trusted to keep his word?

They rode in silence until the barn came into sight.

"Is it okay if I give Star a pedicure while you're on the phone, Mom?"

More than okay. It would give Sarah an opportunity to talk to Jace alone. "That's a great idea."

"I can take Thor." Addie flashed a grin that encompassed both Sarah and Jace. "I'll brush his mane, but I don't think he'll like sparkly hooves."

Jace grinned back as he dismounted and Sarah sucked in a quiet breath. He'd barely smiled when they'd met, but here was the source of Addie's engaging grin.

Addie led Star and Thor into the barn and Sarah opened the gate so Autumn could join the herd. Then she turned toward Jace.

"You said you weren't going to push yourself on Addie."

"I didn't…but…she was going on a trail ride. Alone."

Was Sarah imagining it, or was there a hint of censure in his voice now?

"Addie has been riding since she was four years old. She knows the rules. Stay on the trail. Don't cross the bridge."

"But climbing trees is okay?"

Sarah met Jace's gaze.

"It is when she's with me."

Emphasis on the *me*.

Jace had taken one look at Sarah's expression when he'd seen her astride Autumn and knew he was in trouble. Now he'd managed to insult her, too.

"I'm sorry." Better put that out there right away. "But even experienced riders can run into trouble. At least, that's what I've been told."

By Sarah.

The flash of summer lightning in her eyes before she looked away told Jace that she remembered.

"You should have asked me first."

Jace traced Sarah's profile with his eyes, paused when he saw the set of her chin.

Yes, he should have. But his protective instincts had kicked in when Addie said she was going riding.

"Am I swooping again?"

"Yes." No hesitation.

"So." Jace drew out the word. "What you're saying is that I can't be a helicopter parent."

Sarah's lips flattened again and Jace realized what he'd said.

He wasn't a parent. A parent—a *dad*—was a guy who changed diapers and walked the floor at midnight. Wiped noses and bandaged skinned knees. Sat through school concerts and cheered from the bleachers during sporting events.

He was the guy who'd left Sarah to do all those things—plus a gazillion others—on her own.

How do I make up for that, God?

A popular song filtered through the open windows and Addie joined in, belting out the chorus at a decibel level that would have made the artist proud.

"She's pretty amazing, Sarah. You've done a great job."

Tears banked in her eyes but she blinked them away.

"Maggie had a lot to do with that," she murmured. "She'd never had kids, but she was so patient. Wise. Maggie always knew what to do. What to say."

"True," Jace said softly. Because it had seemed that way to him, too. "But I'm thinking Addie got her sparkle, the way she looks at the world…as if she's expecting something good to happen…that came from you."

Sarah stared at him. And then pivoted toward the cabin.

"I—I have to go."

Why? Because he'd complimented her?

Or because he'd pointed out something she already knew about her daughter? The one he'd met less than a week ago?

I keep messing things up, Lord.

Maybe he should talk to the one person other than Maggie who'd always helped Jace get his head on straight.

The chances of Mason answering the phone were slim, so Jace was getting ready to leave a voicemail when he heard a real voice on the other end.

"I hope you're calling to tell me that you're on your way."

"Not exactly." Jace bypassed the lodge and walked toward the cabin he and Ian had shared with one of the volunteer counselors. A sneaky move on Maggie's part, because the guy was the son of missionary parents who quoted scripture in his sleep. The first few weeks after his arrival, Jace had slept with a pillow over his head.

It was God's sense of humor—and perfect timing—that had

placed him in the barracks with Mason Sinclair during his first tour. Mason, a pastor's kid who knew the lyrics to every praise and worship song and belted them out in the shower.

Jace had wanted to smother *him* with a pillow.

Instead, they'd become best friends. He and Mason were the same age, but Mason had given his life to Christ at the age of seven. A spiritual grown-up in the faith compared to Jace, who was still taking those first stumbling baby steps when they'd met.

The screen door was unlocked, and Jace sank into the wicker chair on the porch, pretty sure it was the same one he'd sat in ten years ago while plotting how to escape Four Arrows.

"I'm still here."

"And where is that? Because the only intel I got was that you had to make a quick stop and check on a friend. That was almost a week ago."

Well, a lot could happen in a week. And a decade. In a decade, a baby could grow into a freckle-faced girl who looked at Jace like he was a hero for answering her plea for help.

What would she think if she found out that Jace was the one who'd walked out on them?

"A friend... Maggie...passed away."

Silence preceded a low groan. "Aw, man. I'm sorry, Jace. Of course you had to stay for the funeral."

"Maggie died three years ago." Jace pushed a hand through his hair. "I'm still here because I found out that I...I have a daughter."

The silence lasted longer this time.

"Did you just say you have a daughter?"

"Addie." Jace realized he didn't even know her middle name. "She's ten years old."

"Her mom..." Mason hesitated. "Is she the one who passed away?"

The thought made Jace's gut clench. "No, Sarah is living at Four Arrows."

He hadn't given Mason many details about the summer he'd spent at camp, hadn't spoken about Sarah at all, but his friend had obviously filed away the few he'd shared.

"That's the camp where you stayed before boot camp?"

"Right."

"Are you going to make me keep guessing, or can you just use the words I know you have stored in that thick head of yours and tell me what's going on?"

Jace did. He started with the day Pastor Gillis had dropped him off at the camp. When Maggie Malone stepped out of the lodge and welcomed an angry, disillusioned kid with the same words she spoke over every camper, counselor and volunteer who came to Four Arrows.

Are you ready for an adventure?

Because that's how Maggie had looked at life. On every path, there were surprises—and challenges—along the way. It wasn't always smooth—sometimes it was so difficult you were tempted to quit—but the things you experienced along the way were worth it.

Jace didn't leave anything out. He told Mason about the visit from Sarah's father. That he'd severed their relationship and set Sarah free to pursue her goals.

Through it all, Mason didn't say a word. No huffs of indignation or condemnation. Jace had spent enough time in his friend's company to know the silence meant he was praying.

Finally, Jace got to the end and expelled a breath.

"So…what do I do?"

A chuckle followed Jace's question. "You already did it, dude. You stayed. Now it's time to see what *God* is going to do."

Chapter Six

Sarah caught a glimpse of her reflection in the truck's rear-view mirror and winced. There was a smudge of dirt on her cheek and pieces of straw poked out of her hair like the quills on a porcupine.

No point pulling them out now. Not when she still had to unload the bales marked for the archery range. She did try to scrape off the dirt with the back of her hand but only ended up making it worse.

No sparkle that Sarah could see, although the shadows underneath her eyes put some color in her face.

And why was she even looking for a…a sparkle anyway?

Because the comment Jace had made after she'd scolded him for accompanying Addie on the trail ride had lodged in her head.

I'm thinking Addie got her sparkle, the way she looks at the world as if she's expecting something good to happen… from you.

Inexplicably, tears scalded the backs of Sarah's eyes and she blinked them away.

Is that how Jace had seen her back then? He'd teased her often enough about her attitude when he'd called her Miss Blue Skies and Sunshine.

And when had she stopped expecting the good and had started to prepare herself for the worst, instead of hoping for the best? When Jace had walked away from her without a backward glance? When her father had given her an ultimatum that if she kept the baby, she'd be on her own? After Maggie died?

Sarah loved working with the horses, but relating to people? That was Maggie's gift. If her friend were still here, the three cancellations would have been filled with three phone calls.

She tapped the brake to let a squirrel cross the road and adjusted the air-conditioning.

Fortunately, Addie had been invited to a friend's house after church, leaving Sarah free to concentrate on one of the projects that required time and a little sweat. What Sarah really wanted to do was go on a long trail ride, but dealing with the most current crisis had pushed other items further down her to-do list.

She'd texted Jace, asking him to mow the archery range, and calculated that he would be finished and onto the next project—replacing a torn screen in the porch on the arts and crafts building—by the time she drove out to set up the targets.

Her calculations were off by mere minutes. Seconds even.

When Sarah turned off the service road onto the archery range, Jace was standing beside the mower, tanned and fit, a warrior in faded jeans and a T-shirt, surveying the field he'd just conquered with a smile on his face.

The smile expanded when he spotted the truck and Sarah's heart lifted as if it had forgotten Jace had crushed it and tossed it aside as carelessly he would a paper cup.

Sarah aimed toward the small storage shed to put some distance between them, but Jace was waiting there as she parked the truck.

"I don't remember the archery range being this big."

It wasn't a complaint. The rumble of satisfaction in Jace's voice told Sarah that he enjoyed a challenge.

Sure, he does, an inner voice chided. *That's how he saw you.*

Because Sarah had tried to avoid him then, too, even though she'd been drawn to Jace like the proverbial moth to a flame. The more time they'd spent together, the more Sarah caught glimpses of the Jace no one else knew. That he'd opened up and shared some of his past, his uncertainty about the future, had made her feel special. In Sarah's mind, they were a couple, but Jace had been only looking out for himself.

"Because you didn't have to mow it back then," Sarah pointed out. She walked around the truck and unlocked the tailgate.

"Maggie didn't trust me with anything that had an engine. I think she was afraid I'd take off."

"I should have given you the keys to my car."

Sarah regretted the words the moment she said them. If she hadn't met Jace, she wouldn't have Addie. Her daughter hadn't been planned but she'd been loved—wanted—from the moment Sarah had discovered that another heart beat next to hers.

A shadow skimmed across the surface of Jace's face.

"Sarah—"

"I have to set up the targets before Addie gets home." Sarah's emotions were too raw for another trip down memory lane.

She plucked the pair of work gloves that dangled from the back pocket of her jeans and slid them on.

Without being asked, Jace grabbed one of the bales from the bed of the truck.

"I've got this," Sarah said quickly. "You can start on the screens."

"Already done." Jace foiled her plot to send him on his way and grabbed another bale. "I'm free the rest of the afternoon."

Jace set the last hay bale in place. Out of the corner of his eye, he caught Sarah slip off a glove and rub the small of her back.

Yeah. Well, he was feeling the burn, too, but it wasn't from setting up targets.

Sarah's comment had Jace doubting whether Mason was right about staying.

He wanted to reduce her stress level, not add to it.

He also wanted to smooth away the furrow between her brows and hear her laugh.

The Sarah Crosse he'd met ten years ago had laughed a lot.

Okay, mostly at him, when he'd attempted activities that other kids had mastered well before they'd turned eighteen. Like swimming. Paddling a canoe.

Archery.

After the bales were unloaded, Sarah had left Jace alone to set them up and ducked into the storage shed, an effective way of making sure he didn't pick up the conversation where they'd left off. With her admitting she wished they'd never met.

Jace positioned himself in the doorway. Because he was as skilled at strategy as he was at flying helicopters.

Sunlight streamed through windows caked with spring pollen—another thing to add to the list—and ignited copper sparks in the wisps of strawberry blond hair that framed Sarah's face.

She stood in front of a wooden table scarred from age, sorting the bows into two piles.

"Some of these need to be restrung," she said without looking at him. "Or replaced."

"I finished setting up the targets, but I'm not sure they're in the right position," Jace said.

"I can check in a few minutes."

"Or we can run a quick test."

Jace removed one of the quivers from a hook on the wall and Sarah glanced over her shoulder.

"The last time we were here, you beat me," he said. "It's only fair I get another chance to prove myself."

Something kindled in Sarah's green eyes but it wasn't anger. For the first time, Jace felt a stab of hope.

And then she started sorting again.

"I don't have time."

And that was exactly why Jace grabbed another quiver. Because if anyone needed to do something simply for the fun of it, and not because it was an item to be checked off her to-do list, it was Sarah.

"Come on. Or are you feeling rusty?"

Jace was goading her and she knew it, but he wasn't going to give up. Sarah was the one who'd taught an awkward city kid how to use a bow and arrow so he could hold his head high among the junior campers.

His skills had improved over the summer, but it wasn't often that he'd bested Sarah in a competition.

"Fine." Jace's triumph was short-lived as she chose a bow from the table. "The first one who hits the bull's-eye wins. Game over."

She took the quiver and swept passed him.

Jace followed, trying not to smile.

Game over?

Nope.

Mission accomplished.

Sarah was feeling rusty. Rusty and already regretting that she'd agreed to this.

And why had she?

Because she'd never been able to resist Jace when he'd gotten that mischievous gleam in his eyes, that's why.

And because Sarah had originally been the one to coax Jace onto the archery field instead of the other way around.

The camp's Fourth of July celebration was three days of nonstop fun and friendly competitions. No one was granted immunity. Everyone from the camp nurse to the volunteer dishwasher was expected to participate.

Jace hadn't been happy when he'd found out about it. Sarah had discovered him behind the lodge, taking out his frustration by turning a stack of helpless logs meant for firewood into kindling.

"I'm not one of the campers," he'd growled to Sarah. "If I

liked making a fool of myself, I would have turned in the poem I wrote for Senior English."

Sarah might have laughed if she hadn't realized what Jace had just admitted. She'd seen Ian and Rae take out the canoes and occasionally join in a game of sand volleyball. Jace shunned the group activities and disappeared for hours, exploring the trails.

She'd assumed he preferred to be alone. Until that moment, it hadn't occurred to Sarah that the summer activities she'd grown up with might be foreign to him.

"You don't have to participate in everything," Sarah had told him. "Just sign up for one event that looks like fun."

"Fun." He'd given *her* a look then, but Sarah wasn't intimidated by Jace's scowls.

"You could do the obstacle course...or archery." She'd looked pointedly at the axe embedded in the chopping block. "You seem to have a pretty good aim."

"I've never tried it," Jace muttered.

"I'll teach you," Sarah had offered. "It's not that hard."

To her astonishment, Jace had agreed. They'd met at the range early the next morning, when the campers were on a scavenger hunt, so they wouldn't have an audience.

Sarah had turned the lesson into a game by writing the names of all the activities Jace had complained about on the targets. By the end of the hour, they'd both been laughing so hard, Sarah barely had the strength to pull the string back. That was the only reason Jace had won, and Sarah had presented him with a prize—a certificate good for a free ice cream treat at the General Store.

He'd shown up at the stable when Sarah was getting ready to leave for the day with a hot fudge sundae and two spoons.

She'd told herself it wasn't a good idea to spend so much time with him. Jace would be leaving at the end of the summer and Sarah had a feeling he'd take her heart with him when he left.

And she'd been right.

Sarah notched an arrow. Focused on the target instead of the man standing beside her.

Because nothing had changed. Jace might be Addie's father, but he would leave again. And Sarah's heart wasn't the only one she had to protect.

"You first, Robin."

Jace had called her Robin Hood the first time Sarah had stepped up to the line and hit the bull's-eye twice in a row.

Out of the corner of her eye, Sarah saw that roguish smile again.

Yes. This was a very bad idea. Because Jace seemed as determined to revisit the past as she was trying to hold the memories at bay.

Jace pretended to sneeze as Sarah released the arrow. It missed the target she'd been aiming for and lodged in the hay bale beside it.

She couldn't say a word. Not when she'd been guilty of the same thing. Jace had complained about having to take part in the Fourth of July competition, but then he'd gone and turned her tutorial lesson into one, leaving Sarah with no choice but to retaliate. Was he remembering all the lessons that followed? When Sarah would cheat a little just to see if she could make him smile?

She stepped back. "Your turn."

Jace notched an arrow. Paused to look at her. "How's my stance?"

Sarah checked out his grip on the bow and the way his body was positioned. Cleared her throat. "Fine."

More than fine. Jace was still lean, but the military had honed his muscles in the same way it had honed his ability to focus.

Before Sarah could blink, his arrow had disappeared into the center of the target.

"I've still got it." He grinned. "Back to you."

Sarah's arrow went wide again and Jace hadn't even sneezed.

"I could write *talent night* on the target," he offered.

"How did you—" She stopped, not sure she wanted to know how *Jace* had known it was her least favorite activity at camp.

"You have a tell."

"A tell."

"You nibble on your bottom lip when you're nervous."

And now Jace's gaze dropped to her lips.

Sarah swallowed hard. "That's because I didn't *have* any talents," she confessed.

Instead of nodding in agreement, Jace's brows shot up. "You're kidding me, right? You had mad cowgirl skills and I watched you settle disputes between middle school girls like a seasoned negotiator. You're a good listener. Patient. And you lip-synch so well, no one can tell you're not really singing."

Sarah stared at him, speechless. She didn't think anyone had noticed. Still, none of the things Jace mentioned, even if they were true, had transitioned well to the stage. She'd preferred to stay in the background, but volunteers were expected to take part in the group activities, and the weekly talent nights were the only thing she'd dreaded.

"No one was supposed to notice," she murmured.

"I notice everything about you."

Notice?

Jace wasn't talking about the past now. And the fact that Sarah wanted to believe him warned her they were moving into dangerous ground.

"The targets are fine." She backed away from him. "Thanks again for your help but… I have to go."

Now. Before she fell for him all over again.

Jace walked up to the door of Sarah's cabin.

This might be a total crash and burn, like his attempt to get Sarah to have fun that afternoon, but a guy had to try.

He knocked on the screen door with his elbow and it swung open.

"Jace!" Addie's eyes lit up at the sight of him. She wore a

canvas apron splotched with paint over her T-shirt and shorts and there was a smear of yellow on her cheek.

"I have something for you and your mom, but I'm not going to stay—"

"Mom!"

Addie's reflexes were obviously superior to his, because she'd grabbed Jace's hand and proceeded to tow him inside before he could protest.

Sarah's cabin was larger than most of the others, with a stone fireplace and a breakfast nook off the kitchen, but Maggie's apartment was twice the size and would give them more space.

Why weren't she and Addie living there?

Sarah sat in a wooden rocker in the miniscule living room, a laptop balanced on her knees. The flannel shirt she'd worn at the archery range was draped over the back of the chair, revealing a bright pink T-shirt. The words "Ice cream. Repeat." were silk-screened on the front.

Jace took that as a sign from God.

"Jace is here," Addie announced, even though less than ten feet separated them.

Sarah stood up quickly and set the laptop aside. It was impossible to get a read on what she thought about his unsanctioned visit, but it was clear he'd interrupted something. A low coffee table in front of the fireplace was shrouded in newspaper, jars of paint and brushes scattered across the surface.

"I'm sorry about the mess." Sarah had tracked his gaze. "Addie is in the middle of a project."

"I'm painting rocks."

Was the sense of wonder that Addie's smiles stirred inside of Jace ever going to go away?

Jace didn't think so.

A child.

His child.

That stirred a sense of wonder, too.

"What? You ran out of paper?" he teased.

"No!" Addie's gurgle of laughter wrapped around Jace's heart and squeezed. "I hide them along the trail for the campers to find. Maggie always said that pleasant words are sweet to the soul and—" She paused and her brows dipped together.

"Health to the bones," Sarah murmured. "It's a verse in Proverbs that Maggie liked to quote, but Addie took it a step further and created a scavenger hunt of sorts."

"Because a person could find the right word at exactly the right time," Addie added.

Jace couldn't tell Addie—or Sarah—that he'd been that person.

The rock he'd discovered half buried in the dirt and leaves now had a place of honor on the writing desk, where Jace could see it every day.

TRUST.

That's what had given him the courage to show up at Sarah's door without an invitation. Wisdom told Jace that now was the time to hand over the bag and walk away.

"Here." Jace presented it to Addie with a wink. "But you have to share."

"Ice cream!" Addie spotted the logo stamped on the paper bag and hugged it against her chest. "Awesome!"

The General Store hadn't been restocked, so Jace had raided the walk-in freezer in the cafeteria looking for ice cream bars. The only thing his search had yielded was a box of ground beef patties. Fortunately, the Sweet Shanty, a combination candy, coffee and ice cream shop in Crosse Creek, had already opened its doors for the summer tourist season.

"I'll be right back."

Jace realized Addie must have misinterpreted his statement about sharing because she dashed into the kitchen and returned a moment later with not two, but three colorful ceramic bowls.

"I can't stay," he said, backing toward the door. "The ice cream is for you and your mom."

Addie stopped. "You have to!" she protested. "Doesn't he, Mom?"

"Of course," Sarah murmured.

Not the most enthusiastic response, but Jace would take it.

"You can't juggle the ice cream and the bowls." Sarah took charge and extracted the dishes from Addie's arms. "Jace... there's a napkin holder on the kitchen counter. Spoons in the top left drawer. We can eat outside at the picnic table."

He retrieved both and followed them out the back door. Tried to hide his surprise.

The trees created a natural fence around a small flagstone patio. A weathered picnic table anchored the space. An iron trellis was the headboard for a raised flower bed and empty terra-cotta pots were ready for planting. A string of solar lights winding through the arbor winked like fireflies now that the sun had started to set. In the middle of the busy camp, Sarah had managed to carve out a private retreat.

As welcoming as it looked, the rustic setting wasn't what Jace had pictured for her. Neither was a cabin with barely enough room to change your mind. Was Sarah happy here? Or was she fulfilling an obligation to Maggie?

Questions Jace doubted Sarah would answer. At least, not if he was the one asking.

God, what do I have to do so she'll trust me again?

The countdown to the camp's opening was getting closer every day, and it was getting more difficult to obey the nudge to wait.

Addie pulled the cardboard containers out of the bag and held one up to read the label.

"You got cookies and cream!" Her eyes glowed. "How did you know that's Mom's favorite kind?"

Because ice cream had been the prize for whoever got the

most bull's-eyes during Jace's archery lessons. A tradition Jace
had started the first time he'd challenged Sarah to a tournament-
for-two. Whoever lost had to buy the other person an ice cream
bar from the General Store. Jace had lost the first three times,
but it meant spending time with Sarah, so it felt like he'd won.

Jace slanted a look at Sarah, not sure how to answer. But
even though she must have heard Addie's question, she wouldn't
look at him as she divided up spoons and napkins.

"I'm a good guesser?" When in doubt, answer a question
with a question.

Addie grinned. "What did you get for me?" She plucked the
small white container from the bag and read the sticker on the
top. "Mint chocolate chip."

A look of disappointment, so fleeting that anyone else might
have missed it, crossed Addie's face.

"Not your favorite, huh?" Jace should have gone with his gut
and picked Blue Moon. But that was *his* favorite, so it hadn't
seemed right.

"No," Addie said quickly. "I like it."

She didn't.

And suddenly, Jace felt like he'd failed an important mission.

Because a dad should know his daughter's favorite flavor of
ice cream.

Anger rolled through Jace. Not at Sarah. At himself. If he'd
been a different person—someone who didn't wreck everything he touched, who deserved a woman like Sarah—maybe
he wouldn't have missed the first ten years of Addie's life.

He watched Addie dip her spoon into the ice cream and take
a delicate bite. Nope. Definitely not a fan of mint.

"If you'd gone with me—" not that Sarah would ever allow
Jace to take Addie out for ice cream "—what would you have
chosen?"

"Blue Moon, probably. But this is good," Addie hastened
to add.

It wasn't like ice cream preferences were hardwired into a person's DNA, but for some reason, that made Jace feel worse.

What else did he and Addie have in common other than the color of their eyes?

And would he ever get the chance to find out?

Not when you keep breaking the rules.

First, he'd accompanied Addie on a trail ride. Showing up unannounced was probably strike two in Sarah's eyes.

"I have a few things to do before it gets dark." Now who was using their to-do list as an excuse to run? "You ladies enjoy your ice cream."

"But...don't you want to stay longer?"

He did. That was the problem. But Sarah's silence told Jace that he'd overstayed his welcome already. And saying good-night was better than a goodbye.

Chapter Seven

Sarah washed the empty ice cream bowls and wiped some splotches of paint off the table. Addie had finished painting the rocks and they were lined up in a neat row, conveying their cheerful messages in an array of pinks, yellows, blues and greens.

JOY. HOPE. PEACE. HI, BEAUTIFUL. COURAGE. SMILE. BE THANKFUL. PRAY BIG.

Addie had told Jace the rocks were for the campers, but Sarah needed to embrace those words, too.

PRAY BIG.

Sarah's gaze lingered on the heart-shaped rock. She hardly prayed at all anymore.

There was just so much to do…and it wasn't like God could give her extra hours in a day. Or another pair of hands.

But He'd sent Jace.

Although the man felt more like a test than a blessing.

"Mom?" Addie's husky voice tugged at Sarah. Addie was framed in the doorway to her bedroom, wearing the nightgown that had fit six months ago but now looked a size too small. Sarah made a silent note to do some online shopping soon. Her girl was growing up. Too fast.

"I thought you were asleep."

"Is Jace… Do you think he's mad at me?" The question tumbled out in a rush.

"Mad?" Sarah echoed. "Of course not, Ads. Why would you say that?"

"He didn't eat any ice cream." Addie flopped down on the couch and pulled her knees against her chest. "Maybe he could tell I didn't like mint chocolate chip and I hurt his feelings."

Sarah released a slow breath as she sat down beside Addie. "You didn't say or do anything to hurt Jace's feelings."

So, Addie had noticed his rather abrupt departure, too. But Sarah knew it didn't have anything to do with ice cream. If he was angry with anyone, it would be Sarah. She was the one who'd kept him from his daughter for the last ten years.

No. She hadn't kept them apart. Jace had *left*. Something that Sarah was trying hard not to forget when Jace seemed equally as determined to make her relive the past. Challenging her on the archery field. Showing up with an ice cream "trophy" even though their last competition had ended with her forfeiting. And running away.

"Did you know Jace when he lived here?"

While Addie's first question had taken Sarah by surprise, the second one stripped the air from her lungs.

"Why do you ask?" she hedged.

"The Sweet Shanty has thirty-two flavors of ice cream, and he picked out your favorite one."

Sarah's mouth had gone dry. She couldn't lie to her daughter, but she couldn't tell her whole truth, either.

"Yes, he lived here one of the summers I volunteered."

"I knew it." Addie's brow furrowed.

Jace claimed that Sarah had a "tell," and that small wrinkle between her daughter's brows told Sarah she was thinking hard about something. But Sarah had reached her quota of surprises for the day. She didn't give Addie the opportunity to ask any more questions.

"Bedtime," Sarah said. "Dr. Callahan left a message that he'll be here bright and early tomorrow morning for the wellness checks." She wrapped Addie in a hug and then nudged her toward the bedroom.

"'Night." A yawn punctuated the word and then Addie flashed a grin. "Sweet dreams, jelly beans."

Sarah had been closing the day with those words since Addie was a toddler and it had turned into a game, who would say them first.

Sarah's mind had been on other things. Like archery competitions. And ice cream on hot summer days...

She shook the memories away.

Her dreams would only be sweet if Jace didn't invade them the way he'd been invading her thoughts during the day.

"He's lost a fair amount of weight over the winter, Sarah."

Sarah's heart sank as the veterinarian pressed his stethoscope against Pancakes's belly.

Why hadn't she noticed the gelding's ribs looked a little more defined, now that he'd shed his winter coat?

"There's plenty of hay to go around, but maybe the other horses are pushing him away." Sarah made a note to pay more attention. As congenial as the horses were when it came to interacting with people, there was a pecking order in every herd.

"He's what? Twenty?"

"Twenty-two," Sarah admitted.

"Time flies." Dr. Callahan put away the instrument and patted Pancakes's flank. "Everything sounds fine, but I'll check his teeth. Horses this age can start to have issues."

Pancakes stood patiently during the dental exam. Sarah was the fidgety one. The gelding was one of their best trail horses for beginning riders. Patient and sweet-tempered, he was also one of Sarah's favorites.

"He lost a few teeth since my last visit," Dr. Callahan finally said. "And since no one's designed dentures for our equine seniors, you're going to have to supplement his diet twice a day with pellets and some beet pulp. That way we'll know he's getting enough nutrition. Val at the feed store can put in an order for you."

Sarah knew the dentures comment was the vet's attempt to lighten the news, so she mustered a smile. Hay was expensive enough without adding specialized feed, even if it was only for one horse.

She reached out and rubbed the gelding's nose, feeling guilty she hadn't noticed the weight loss. And that her first thought had been the cost of the new feed.

"I stopped by Timber Ridge," Dr. Callahan said after a moment, referring to a riding stable a few miles from Crosse Creek. Timber Ridge was only open during the summer months, but it was a popular stop for the tourists making their way farther north. "Patti and Tom Jensen asked if I knew anyone who might have some seasoned trail horses for sale. They're interested in expanding their stable."

Had he read her mind? They'd gotten to know each other well after Sarah had moved in with Maggie, and the veterinarian had made a point to stop by and check on Sarah at least once a month after Maggie had died.

Sarah bit her lip. Remembered what Jace had said and immediately released it again.

"Would they have time to deal with Pancakes and a special diet, though?" As it was, Sarah would have to feed the horse separately from the rest of the herd from now on.

Dr. C cleared his throat. "I wasn't only thinking about Pancakes. You've got a great bunch of riding horses, Sarah. I'm sure any or—" he added carefully "—all of them would be of interest to the Jensens. Tom mentioned he'd pay top dollar."

Sarah's gaze cut to the round pen, where the horses waited placidly for their turn with the vet. She'd been involved with Four Arrows since she was fifteen years old and knew every one of the horses by name. Knew their quirks and temperaments. Delivered foals that had grown up with the campers.

She teetered between laughing as if Dr. Callahan had made another joke, or breaking down and crying because he'd dared to acknowledge what Sarah had been denying for months. The horses had become the largest drain on the camp's resources.

The bill for the horses' annual wellness checks today would take a sizable chunk from the bank account.

But shutting down the equine camps—selling the horses— would break Addie's heart. And hers. Sarah couldn't imagine parting with Pancakes. Star. Autumn. Any of the horses, really.

But with the latest cancellation, Sarah was running out of options.

Another sign that Maggie should have entrusted her legacy to someone else.

Sarah hadn't told anyone that things weren't going well at the camp, but Dr. Callahan was an intelligent man. And a compassionate one. Sarah couldn't get angry with him for offering a solution.

She glanced over her shoulder to make sure Addie wasn't in earshot. She'd offered to muck out stalls after they'd rounded up the horses and secured them in the round pen for the veterinarian's visit.

"Thank you for letting me know," she murmured. "I'll… think about…a name."

Dr. Callahan's hand clamped down on her shoulder. "You're doing a great job, Sarah. But Four Arrows was Maggie's dream. It doesn't have to be yours. If there's something else you wanted to pursue, she would understand."

Sarah nodded, unable to talk around the knot that had formed in her throat.

The camp wasn't a burden, it was home. And she wanted Four Arrows to succeed. Wanted to keep Maggie's dream alive. Sarah just wasn't sure she was the right person for the job.

A low growl of thunder in the distance drew their attention to the sky.

Sarah hoped the storm bearing down on them wouldn't cause as much damage as the last one.

"That's my cue." The veterinarian began packing up his bag. "Don't hesitate to call if you need anything."

Sarah wasn't good at asking for help. Sometimes she wondered if that was part of the problem. Maggie hadn't hesitated to contact her lengthy list of volunteers if the camp had a need, but it didn't come easily to Sarah. Her father had always said that asking for help was a sign of weakness. And confiding in anyone about the camp's financial problems would be akin to admitting she was failing at the most important task Maggie had entrusted to her.

Jace watched the veterinarian's truck rattle down the road as he set the last window in place.

Just in time, too. A drop of rain splashed on his bare arm. And then another. He moved the tools onto the screened-in porch and jogged back to the lodge before the slow trickle escaping through the seams in the clouds turned into a deluge.

The moment the front door closed behind Jace, his internal radar went off. He paused, took a slow sweep of his surroundings. At first glance, nothing looked out of place, but his instincts had been honed to focus in on the smallest of details. A change in the air. A rustle in the trees. Or, in this case, the sense that he wasn't alone.

The cabin Jace had been working on was located right between the barn and the lodge, so he would have noticed if Sarah had been here. He noticed everything about Sarah. The way her eyes softened whenever she looked at Addie. The guarded expression on her face when she looked at *him*. Something Jace was determined to change…

He took another step forward and a soft thump coming from Maggie's office told Jace he hadn't been imagining things.

He'd heard noises in the attic several days ago. Maybe whatever critter had been living there had finally found a way inside.

Jace placed himself squarely in the center of the doorway to block any attempts at escape...

A soft squeal broke the silence and a tower of books on the floor toppled over. Several of them slid across the hardwood floor, past the desk, and landed next to Jace's feet.

"Jace," Addie gasped, her eyes wide as she clutched a book to her chest.

He wasn't sure if her reaction stemmed from surprise or guilt.

Color rose in her cheeks like mercury in a thermometer.

Definitely guilt.

Jace wasn't sure how to handle this. The lodge wasn't his private residence, but he doubted there was anything in Maggie's office that would be of interest to a ten-year-old girl.

"Were you looking for something?"

Addie shrugged, even though the evidence lay right at Jace's feet. He bent down and scooped up the books.

He recognized the covers instantly. At the end of every year, Maggie had collected all the candid shots she'd taken of the campers who'd visited Four Arrows and sent them to a company that compiled them into a special album. Jace knew this because he'd dodged her camera lens on more than one occasion. He wasn't a camper or a volunteer like Sarah. He was a charity case. An outsider. He didn't belong in one of Maggie's photo books.

Jace's gaze landed on the other volumes scattered on the floor.

"I suppose your mom is in a lot of those," he ventured.

Sarah had mentioned once that she'd started volunteering at the camp when she was a freshman in high school.

Another shrug.

Jace had known his daughter a week, but it was long enough to know something wasn't right.

He suddenly realized Maggie's volunteers had occasionally confiscated her camera and turned the lens on her. Addie was only seven when Maggie had passed away. Maybe she wanted to page through the books so she wouldn't forget the other woman who'd played a significant role in her life.

And Jace had interrupted her.

The lights flickered. Through the window, Jace saw a flash of lightning.

He crossed the space between them and handed Addie the books. Smiled. "You better get home or you'll be stuck here until the storm blows over."

Jace wouldn't mind spending more time with his daughter, but Sarah would. After last night, he didn't want there to be a strike three.

"Okay." Addie bent down to retrieve one of the books scattered on the floor.

"I'll do that—"

"No! I've got it!" Before Jace could join in the cleanup, Addie was scooping up the rest and stuffing them back on the shelf.

Jace took the hint and retreated to his room. When the front door closed a few minutes later, he glanced out the window just in time to see Addie dashing toward the barn.

The rain had put a damper on his plan to replace another set of windows, but Jace had noticed some minor repairs that would keep him busy inside the lodge.

No amount of busywork would prevent him from thinking about Sarah, though.

Two weeks, Jace had told her. Time was running out and Sarah would expect him to keep his promise and leave.

But saying goodbye again—to her and to Addie—was one that Jace didn't want to keep.

Chapter Eight

There was no getting around it. Sarah had bills to pay and phone calls she didn't want to make while Addie was holed up in her bedroom, a mere ten feet away. Rain still fell in a steady drizzle, making it the perfect afternoon to put in some office hours.

Except the office happened to be located in the lodge.

And so was Jace.

She rapped on Addie's bedroom door. Turned the handle and frowned.

"Ads?" She jiggled it again. "Why is the door locked?"

It opened a few seconds later. Well, a crack anyway. The only thing Sarah could see was one big brown eye. "What's up, Mom?"

"You tell me." Sarah's maternal radar shifted to high alert. "Did you let Maisey up on the bed again?"

The door opened another inch.

"Nope, she's over there." Addie pointed to the dog, who was curled up in her favorite spot underneath the window. "I was just, um, reading."

That explained her odd behavior. When Addie became engrossed in a book, she didn't want to be disturbed. Sarah was the same way.

"I have some work to do on the computer," Sarah told her. "It will only take an hour or so, but if you want to come with me…"

Addie was already shaking her head. "I'll stay here with Maisey."

Sarah tried to hide her relief. Now that her junior detective had discovered that Sarah and Jace had known each other at camp, she was afraid Addie would seize the opportunity to spend time with Jace and ask questions that Sarah had managed to avoid.

But she couldn't avoid them forever.

Jace had changed. Sarah couldn't deny it. It wasn't only the confidence he wore as comfortably as his faded jeans. She looked in his eyes and saw…peace. He wasn't pretending to be patient. Helpful. Funny. Those qualities were part of the man he'd become.

And they only made him more appealing. Not only to Addie, but to Sarah. There was the danger. Because the changes she saw in Jace didn't change the fact that he would be leaving.

"Can I have a snack while you're gone?"

"I'll make popcorn when I get back," Sarah promised.

"And a movie?"

Sarah tipped her head. "How about this? Let's set up the projector in the barn and make sure the equipment is working."

Movie nights had always been a hit with the campers. An ancient and slightly temperamental projector turned the barn into a theater, complete with hay-bale seating and an old-fashioned popcorn machine set up in the corner.

The rain was supposed to linger through the evening hours. Sarah could spend time with Addie *and* cross an item off her to-do list.

"Okay! Can we invite Jace?"

Sarah should have seen that coming. In Addie's eyes, Jace was the hero who'd responded to her plea for help. The man who showed up at the door with ice cream. Teased her.

For ten years, Sarah had convinced herself that Addie was better off without a father who'd abandoned them.

Maggie had brought it up—once. Gently questioned Sarah's decision not to tell Jace about the baby. It was the only time Sarah remembered pushing back against her friend. Not because Maggie was wrong...because Sarah was afraid.

Yes, Jace might have come back to Crosse Creek. But what if he'd ended up resenting her? Sarah's father had.

A month after Sarah had told him that she was pregnant, her father accepted a position with a global nonprofit that needed doctors. Everyone in Crosse Creek had thought he was sacrificing a successful medical practice for those in poverty, but Sarah knew the truth.

Her father had assumed she would put the baby up for adoption and continue with her plan to go to college. Without her knowledge or consent, he'd even contacted an adoption agency on her behalf.

Sarah had wanted—*needed*—his support, but he'd accused her of throwing her future away after she'd told him that she was keeping her baby. That Sarah hadn't wavered had caused a deeper rift in their relationship. He'd claimed her "mistake" would ruin his standing in their small community.

If it hadn't been for Maggie, Sarah wasn't sure what she would have done. Her father had put her childhood home up for sale, shut down his practice and left town before Addie was born.

It had taken a long time to realize that Franklin Crosse had supported Sarah as long as she'd played the role of the perfect daughter.

"Jace may already have plans." And Sarah had planned on slipping into the office, closing the door and avoiding Jace altogether. "It's your turn to pick the movie," she added, hoping to distract her. "I'll be back soon."

Sarah grabbed her jacket and ducked outside. Jace's truck was parked behind the lodge. She knew he'd been replacing windows in one of the cabins while Dr. Callahan performed the checkups, but the weather would have driven him inside, too.

A weight pressed down on Sarah's chest again as she remembered her conversation with the vet.

But contacting the Jensens, asking a few questions, didn't obligate her in any way.

If another group of campers took the available dates, they could make it through the summer.

Except she was still low on staff. Volunteers. And the cost of repairs had spiked significantly since Maggie had passed away.

Sarah paused as she reached the top step. On the other side of the door, she heard the steady hum of a power tool. Good. If Jace was working on a project, he wouldn't know she was there.

She resisted the urge to knock and slipped inside.

Classic jazz played a backbeat to the sounds coming from the second floor. Sarah knew Jace had chosen the infirmary over Maggie's apartment, but if he'd been making use of the kitchenette, he would have noticed the loose floorboards and the constant drip in the sink.

Sarah ducked into the office.

Maggie hadn't spent much time here. She loved being outdoors, preferred spending time with the volunteers and her campers rather than the office, but that didn't stop the familiar rush of grief.

Sarah dusted the bookshelves and swept the floor once a week, but couldn't bring herself to make any changes. And even though it would make sense as the new camp director to move from the cabin into Maggie's spacious apartment on the second floor, Sarah couldn't bring herself to do that, either.

She sat down at the desk. The computer should have been replaced years ago and Sarah found herself holding her breath until the icons popped up on the screen.

Updating the camp's technology was another thing she couldn't ignore much longer.

She paid the outstanding bills and opened a file with the names of past camp alumni and their phone numbers. The generous gifts from donors who'd had a special connection to Maggie had tapered off since her death, and everything inside Sarah rebelled against reaching out to them. At least for right now.

There'd been lean years before. Sarah had lived there through some of them. Maggie's faith had never wavered, though.

"Four Arrows was God's idea from the get-go," she'd told Sarah. "He'll work it out."

Sarah wanted to believe it. But could He, maybe, work things out a little bit faster?

Which brought her to another phone call she didn't want to make.

The Jensens.

She dialed the number, her pulse spiking higher with every ring.

It was a relief when the call went to voicemail. Sarah left a brief message and hung up.

Maybe she could organize a special fundraiser. Not through phone calls or letters, but with a reunion of sorts. To show people...*what?*

An inner voice mocked the idea.

How neglected the camp looks? An empty stable?

Sarah couldn't think about an empty stable.

Her gaze shifted to the photo on the desk—a selfie Addie had taken of the three of them with Maggie's phone. She'd been even smaller then, with a shorter reach, so the only thing showing was three pairs of eyes and the tops of their heads.

Maggie had loved it. Printed it out and framed it simply because it made her smile.

Sarah closed her eyes.

Oh, she missed her friend. Missed their long talks. Missed Maggie's unshakeable faith and wisdom.

Sarah could use a little of both right now.

* * *

Jace turned off the sander and set it on the table next to the half-eaten grilled cheese sandwich he'd made for lunch.

One project had rolled into another over the course of the afternoon. He'd fixed the squeaky floorboard, tightened the loose hinges on the cabinet doors and sanded off three coats of old paint around the window so he could open it and let some fresh air flow into the kitchen.

Not quite the way Jace had pictured his life after he'd left the service.

"You're a rotorhead," Mason had said. "I can't give you a helicopter, but I have a plane that needs a pilot."

His friend had also promised fly-fishing and white-water rafting. Climbing. A dose of adrenalin every day if Jace came to work for his outfitting and guide business.

A week ago, that had sounded good to Jace.

He opened the window, breathed in the scent of rain mixed with pine.

Seeing Sarah again…meeting Addie…coming back to Four Arrows. Jace couldn't shake the feeling *this* was where he fit.

The problem with that?

Sarah didn't want him here.

He started to gather up his tools and heard a noise coming from the vent in the floor. He shut off the music and zeroed in on the sound. Just when Jace decided it was his imagination, he heard it again.

Maggie's office was directly below the kitchenette.

His lips curved in a smile.

This time, he had the advantage.

Jace avoided the squeaks and creaks on the stairs and saw a light shining underneath the office door. In one swift move, he pushed it open.

"Boo!"

Silence.

Because it was Sarah, not Addie, sitting at the desk. Today, her strawberry blond mane had been captured into a loose top-knot on her head that drew attention to her sculpted features and fern-green eyes.

Her gaze tangled with his as she vaulted to her feet, one hand pressed against her chest.

"Sorry." Jace winced. "I thought Addie had come back."

"Come back?"

"I found her here earlier this morning…" And maybe he shouldn't have said anything, because Sarah was frowning now, proof she didn't know Addie had been at the lodge.

"Here? In Maggie's office? Why?"

She was looking at Jace as if he were somehow to blame.

"I got the impression she was looking for something to read."

Sarah's shoulders relaxed. "Maggie kept every book she ever read from the first grade on. Instead of downsizing, she just added more shelves."

"I believe that." Jace grinned. "She tried to get me to read a book of poetry once. She claimed it would be good for me, but I told her that I'd rather eat a plate of brussels sprouts. So, guess what we had for dinner that night?"

"That was your fault?" Sarah's low laugh arrowed straight through Jace. *More*, he wanted to say. "The campers almost mutinied."

"Maggie's sense of humor." Jace shook his head at the memory. "I haven't tried them since."

"Addie doesn't like…" Sarah's lips pressed together, sealing off the rest of the sentence, but it was too late. Jace had already filled in the blanks.

Like their favorite ice cream flavor, there was something else he and Addie had in common.

Jace decided to steer the conversation onto safer ground.

"How did the wellness checks go?"

Sarah's gaze drifted to the bookshelves again. "Overall, the horses are in great shape."

Overall.

That left room for questions, but Jace wasn't sure how hard to push.

Ten years ago, he could see how attached Sarah was to the horses she'd cared for as a volunteer. He could only imagine how strong that bond had grown now that she was in charge of the entire stable.

He wanted her to confide in him. To be honest about what had put the shadows in her eyes.

Bottom line, though? Jace was afraid she would say it was *him*. He was the one who'd shown up to help and disrupted her life.

But then, his life had been disrupted, too. Jace was still trying to wrap his head around the fact that he had a daughter.

He wanted to know everything there was to know about Addie, but he was afraid to ask. Wasn't sure he even had the right.

"There's a delivery truck arriving tomorrow with kitchen supplies," Sarah was saying. "I have to run some errands in the morning, so could you direct the driver to the cafeteria if I'm not here and help him unload? Some of the supplies are perishables."

"No problem." Jace wondered about the undercurrent of tension in Sarah's voice. She was wearing too many hats. Jace wanted to wrap his arms around her, share the weight of whatever burden Sarah was carrying, but settled for trying to make her smile. "Mrs. Hoffman isn't still in charge of the kitchen, is she? Because I refuse to be an accomplice to a cook who feeds the campers brussels sprouts."

Not only did Sarah *not* smile, a sigh escaped from her lips.

"Usually, but Jean and her husband had a family emergency and can't help out this summer." Sarah paused, but Jace read between the lines. "I'm still trying to find someone to take their place."

"*Their* place?"

"Her husband, Bob, takes care of the grounds." Sarah's smile didn't reach her eyes. "It's a good thing the first group of campers only signed up for one trail ride. I might be working in the kitchen that week."

Jace silently counted the days until the camp's official opening.

"I'm sure they're difficult to replace, but there has to be someone." From what he recalled, Maggie had had a veritable army of volunteers waiting in the reserves, and many of them attended Crosse Creek Community. "Have you talked to your pastor?"

"It's an unpaid, live-in position for twelve weeks," Sarah said stiffly. "Even if someone in town was qualified, I can't imagine they would agree to that."

Jace couldn't help but notice she'd avoided his question.

"Maggie would—"

"Have everything under control. I know." Sarah's hands rolled into fists at her sides.

Whoa.

Where had that come from?

"That's not what I was going to say," Jace said carefully, afraid she'd bolt. "Maggie would have said that God is in control. And He can do more than we can ask or even imagine. I know, because she said it to me on repeat that summer." His lips tipped in a rueful smile. "Probably because she knew it would take a while to sink into my thick skull."

Sarah didn't respond, and Jace was a little unnerved by the intensity of her gaze. Had he overstepped? Was this strike three?

Sarah had been a believer since she was a little girl. What could Jace tell her that she didn't already know?

And yet…there was the nudge again.

"A situation may look impossible, but we have to trust and then...wait," Jace said.

Which, as he knew from the past week, was easier said than done. That's where the trust part came in.

Sarah stared at Jace.

Jace...who'd once shrugged off the existence of a loving God, was reminding her that He was in control. Encouraging her to trust.

His quiet confidence...the peace in his eyes...now Sarah knew its source.

"Sorry." Jace winced. "I don't mean to tell you something that you already know."

Yes, but did she live like she believed it, no matter what the circumstances? Had she prayed about the situation? Or had she been trying to do everything—solve every problem—in her own strength?

"It's all right," Sarah murmured, still stunned that Jace was a believer now.

He didn't hear her. He'd knelt down and was reaching under the desk. When he rose, Sarah saw one of Maggie's photo albums in his hand. Sarah was surprised she hadn't noticed it when she'd sat down at the computer.

"How did that get under there?"

"My fault." Jace dusted off the cover. "Addie had a stack of them on the floor and when I startled her, she jumped and the books scattered. I guess she missed this one."

I'm reading, Addie had said.

Sarah pivoted toward the bookcase and ran her finger along the spines of the albums arranged by date.

"What's wrong?" Jace had stepped closer.

Nothing. Sarah hoped.

She slanted a glance at him. "What did Addie say when you found her here?"

"Not a lot." Jace tipped his head. "Which was kind of odd."

As odd as a locked door.

And Addie's decision to stay at the cabin.

Sarah's heart began to pound in her ears.

"Did she take any albums with her?"

"I'm not sure. I didn't ask any questions. I figured she was missing Maggie and wanted to see some photos of her," Jace explained.

Sarah's gaze dropped to the book in Jace's hands. "Two of them are gone."

And Sarah had a sinking feeling she knew which two.

Jace handed it back and Sarah looked at the date. She shelved it with the rest, saw it tip ever so slightly, proof that her suspicions were correct.

"Addie asked if we'd known each other when you lived here," Sarah said, her voice thin, shaky, even to her own ears. "She isn't looking for pictures of Maggie… She's looking for pictures of you. Or…us."

"But there aren't any." Jace paused, searching her face. "Are there?"

"I don't know." Sarah looked at the gap between the books again. "I never… I didn't look."

Her heart had held enough memories of Jace without seeing them in print.

"Excuse me." Sarah was halfway to the door, terrified of what her curious little detective would discover.

Did Addie already suspect that Jace was her father?

Should she have told her right away?

But Addie had already lost her grandpa and Maggie. Getting to know her dad, only to have him walk out of her life again, would just bring more grief.

Why had Jace come back into their lives? Sarah had moved on. Or at least she'd tried to. Throughout her pregnancy, Sarah had hoped—dreamed—of his return. In her imagination, dozens of scenarios had ended with the three of them becoming a family. But when the weeks turned into months, and the months into years, Sarah had to face reality. Jace had been telling the truth when he'd said that he was looking for fun, not forever.

"Don't panic," she heard Jace say.

"I'm not…but I have to go."

"Wait. Sarah?"

Jace called her name but she didn't look back.

On the way to the cabin, Sarah told herself she was overreacting. But why the secrecy? Sarah wasn't used to Addie keeping things from her.

She dodged puddles in the road as she forced herself to slow from a sprint to a jog.

Low in the trees, the sun broke through the clouds, turning them pink and apricot, a final display that the storm hadn't won before the moon took its place for the night.

Maisey greeted Sarah at the door, tail wagging. Sarah bent down and gave the dog's ears a quick scratch.

Addie's door was closed.

"I'm back." Sarah tried to inject enough cheer to dilute the strain in her voice. "How about a quick trail ride before we start dinner?"

Crickets.

Sarah opened the door—at least it wasn't locked this time— and saw Addie sitting cross-legged on her bed, completely engrossed in the photobook balanced in her lap.

Now she was panicking.

Chapter Nine

❦

"Hey, kiddo."

Addie's head jerked up and color tinted her cheeks. "Mom. I didn't hear you come in."

Obviously.

Sarah studied her daughter's face but didn't see any evidence that Addie had been upset by something she'd found.

"Is that what you've been reading?" Sarah nodded at the book.

The color deepened. "Uh-huh. Do you think… Would Maggie mind?"

"Not at all!" Maybe Jace had been right about why Addie had taken the albums. But as far as Sarah knew, Addie had never expressed an interest in them. Until now. "She only kept them in her office because she didn't want to lose them. If any of the campers wanted a copy of their own, Maggie made sure they got one."

Come to think of it, Sarah had completely forgotten to collect the photos and put them together over the past few years. Between her own responsibilities as head wrangler, and taking on Maggie's role as camp director, taking photographs of the campers had been the last thing on her mind.

Addie glanced down at the book. "There are lots of pictures of Maggie…and you."

"Really?" Sarah's surprise was genuine. The camp was always a buzz of activity. She'd been so busy with the horses, she hadn't noticed Maggie or one of the volunteers taking photos. "I did spend my summers here when I was in high school." She chuckled. "I hope no one snapped a picture of me sitting in a mud puddle because I didn't tighten Dakota's cinch." The gelding still had a habit of holding his breath when Sarah put the saddle on.

A smile rustled at the corners of Addie's lips. "Always expect the unexpected," she said, reciting one of Sarah's Ten Rules for the Trail posted on the wall inside the barn.

Maybe it wouldn't hurt to read through them again. Although Sarah had never expected Jace Marshall to show up at Four Arrows after a ten-year absence.

"What about that trail ride before it gets dark?"

"I didn't look at this one yet."

Sarah gave up and perched on the edge of the bed. Glanced at the date on the spine of the book in Addie's lap and sucked in a breath. It was the summer she'd switched from volunteer to paid staff at the camp. The summer she'd met Jace.

Addie opened the cover. On page one, there was a photo lineup of the full-time summer staff. Sarah's eighteen-year-old self was smiling back at her.

"Head wrangler." Addie read the title underneath Sarah's photograph. "That's so awesome."

"I thought so."

"Will I be head wrangler when I'm eighteen?"

Sarah ignored the stab of pain and forced a smile. "Ask me when you're seventeen-and-a-half."

Addie's nose wrinkled. "Was Jace here that summer?"

All Sarah could do was nod.

Addie began to turn pages. "Are there any pictures of him?"

"I doubt it," Sarah said truthfully. "He spent a lot of time cutting wood for Campfire when he was here."

"Who is this?" Addie's eyes widened as she pointed to a slender girl with turquoise braids standing at the edge of the water.

"Rae Channing." Sarah had tried to befriend the only girl in the trio Maggie had taken in that summer, but in many ways, Rae was as guarded as Jace. Their paths hadn't crossed very often because Sarah spent the majority of her time at the stable or on the trails, while Rae helped out in the kitchen.

Addie repeated the name and squealed. "She gave Maggie a card! When do you think she'll get here?"

Sarah had been afraid this would happen. She hadn't heard a word from Rae and Ian after they'd received Addie's SOS. If the cards had even reached them.

"Addie...people are really busy and we have no idea what they're doing now," Sarah reminded her gently. "They might not be able to help out."

Even if by some chance Rae and Ian were curious about the cards showing up in their mailboxes ten years later, they wouldn't show up at the door unannounced like Jace. Sarah could assure them that the promise they'd made to Maggie did, in fact, have an expiration date and wasn't a lifetime guarantee.

Addie slanted a look at her. "I wish my hair was that color."

A conversation for another day.

Sarah quickly skimmed over the collage of photos on the opposite page.

They must have been taken during one of the talent nights, because the flatbed-trailer-turned-temporary-stage had been hauled out from behind the tool shed and decorated with strings of white lights.

Addie gasped. "Is that you, Mom?"

Sarah stifled a groan.

"Unfortunately. Yes." One of the performances had been canceled at the last minute after the teens stumbled upon a patch of poison ivy, so Maggie had gone around the camp, recruiting volunteers to take their place in the skit. Which involved lip-synching to a humorous country song about opposites.

"Who is he?" Addie pointed at the boy holding the microphone.

"Ian Bradford."

Jace was a loner by choice, but Sarah suspected Ian avoided conversation because of a pronounced stutter. Maggie had had a way of making a person feel like they could accomplish anything, and somehow convinced Ian to be part of the duet.

Ian had worn a tuxedo jacket with velvet lapels that was two sizes too big. Sarah, who'd never liked being the center of attention, had emerged from "wardrobe" in leather chaps, the red cowboy boots she saved for special occasions and a gaudy vest rescued from the lost and found.

They'd won first place, but the only emotion Sarah remembered feeling was disappointment because Jace hadn't been in the audience that night.

"Do you still have those boots?" Addie asked eagerly. "Do you think they'd fit me?"

"Maybe in a few years." Sarah laughed. "They might be in storage somewhere. I can look in the attic—"

"Mom?" Addie had flipped to the next page. "Is…is that Jace?"

Sarah's laughter died in her throat. Because it wasn't only Jace in the photo. Sarah was there, too. They were smiling at each other as they walked down the trail. Holding hands.

Maggie hadn't taken the picture, that much Sarah knew. Afraid one of the volunteers who attended Sarah's church in Crosse Creek would say something to her father, she'd kept their relationship a secret—even from Maggie. Sarah's heart turned over as she studied the photo. They'd been so caught up in the moment, in being together, they'd been oblivious to anything else. Like a person with a camera aimed in their direction.

Addie was staring at Sarah now, her expression confused.

"Y-yes. That's Jace," Sarah managed.

"Did you like each other or something?"

Or something.

Sarah had thought she'd been in love...believed that Jace had loved her, too.

Lord, please...

She wasn't ready for this conversation.

In the silence, Addie drew her own conclusion. "Why did you break up? You're holding hands and you look happy. Jace looks happy, too."

Sarah's gaze shifted to the photo again. They did look happy. But happy didn't always lead to forever.

It was fun...

Jace's last words were burned in Sarah's memory. A permanent scar.

"It was a long time ago, sweetheart. We...we were young."

Sarah saw the exact moment that her bright, inquisitive daughter realized just how young they'd been.

"Mom...is Jace...is he my dad?"

Jace stood frozen in the center of Sarah's tiny living room.

He'd knocked, but no one had answered, so he'd accepted Maisey's wagging tail as an invitation to come in.

Because he'd been worried. Worried about Sarah and worried about Addie and worried about what was happening and why hadn't any of the guys in his unit who'd had kids warned him that parenting felt like stumbling through the dark without night-vision goggles?

The silence that followed Addie's question seemed to last forever.

Would she tell Addie the truth? And how would Addie feel about him now? Would her eyes still light up when he walked into the room? Would she seek out his company?

Or would she feel the same way Sarah did? That he couldn't be trusted?

Maybe Jace should have left when Sarah had asked him to. Staying had stirred up the past and she wouldn't thank him for it. Once again, he'd tried to do the right thing and had messed it all up. Maybe his presence was a complication Sarah didn't need right now.

"Addie—"

"He is, isn't he? Why did he leave? Was it my fault? Didn't Jace… Didn't he want me?"

Jace's heart bottomed out.

From his vantage point, he saw Sarah flinch. She might not want him here, but this was a conversation with Addie that she shouldn't have to have alone.

"I made a mistake."

Two heads swiveled in his direction.

"I'm sorry…" Jace sought out Sarah first. She looked pale, the shadows underneath her eyes more pronounced. His gaze shifted to Addie. "We would have told you sooner, but we weren't sure how to go about it. Sometimes adults have to figure things out, too."

Addie was staring at him, wide-eyed, as if she were seeing him for the first time.

"And it wasn't your fault," he added firmly. "I left at the end of the summer and I…didn't come back."

"You went into the army." In Addie's tremulous smile was a grace Jace didn't deserve.

Oh, Jace really wanted to play the hero card right now and let Addie believe it was duty to his country that had kept him away. But he and Sarah both knew who'd made the most sacrifices, and it wasn't him.

Jace had been so convinced he was doing the right thing, so convinced Sarah was better off without him, he'd signed the enlistment papers and refused to look back.

Sarah stiffened and Jace sent up a silent prayer that he wouldn't say the wrong thing. "I did join the army, but I should have come back. And your mom didn't know how to find me, so she couldn't tell me about you."

"You didn't know about me?" Addie whispered.

"Not until last week, when you told me your birthday."

Addie appeared to be thinking about that.

"I asked about you when I was little because there was a father-daughter dance at school," she murmured. "Mom said you never really had a family and you weren't sure you'd be a good dad."

What Jace remembered declaring was that he never wanted to have children because he'd only mess that up, too.

Jace's throat tightened.

Sarah could have painted him as the villain, the deadbeat dad who'd abandoned them, but she hadn't. Jace didn't deserve that kind of grace from her, either.

"She was right," he said quietly. "I wasn't very good at loving people when I met your mom, but God's been showing me how it's done. If I could go back in time, I'd do things differently, but I can't. All I can do is say I'm sorry…and be here for you now."

Sarah had gone completely still, but Addie jumped off the bed. She launched herself at Jace and her arms circled his neck. For a moment, he couldn't breathe.

"I forgive you," she whispered in Jace's ear. "And I prayed someday my dad would come back."

Jace didn't deserve this. He didn't deserve a second chance with Sarah, either. He realized how deeply he'd hurt her and wanted—no, needed—her forgiveness. Jace had asked God for an opportunity to rebuild Sarah's trust, but now he realized something else.

He wanted to win her love again.

Chapter Ten

"**H**ey, Sarah!" Val grabbed a fifty-pound bag of cracked corn off a dolly and tossed it on the shelf as if it weighed no more than a candy bar. "What's new with you? S'pose you've been busy getting the camp ready for the summer."

Sarah was glad Val supplied her own answer. The *what's new* was a topic she didn't want to share with the owner of the feed store. Or anyone else for that matter, because it involved Jace showing up. Jace insisting on staying. Jace stepping in the night before and shifting all the blame for leaving onto himself, gently explaining to Addie the reason he'd left.

Jace promising Addie he would be here for her now.

Addie hadn't hesitated. Sarah had watched her fly into his arms. She'd whispered something in his ear and even though Sarah couldn't hear, Jace's expression had brought tears to her eyes.

He'd promised Addie he would be here for her now, but *now* was one more week.

Everything had changed…and yet it hadn't.

"…Dr. C mentioned you'd be stopping by," Val was saying. "I put an order in for the feed and it came in yesterday."

"Oh…thank you." Sarah followed Val to the cash register.

Crosse Creek was like any small town. There was no such thing as gossip. It was called sharing information.

"My granddaughter was terrified of horses until she went to

camp and was partnered with Pancakes." Val stripped off her work gloves and tucked them into the front pocket of her Carhartt overalls. "He was the perfect gentleman. A horse like that deserves a little spoiling in their golden years." She winked. "Like the rest of us, heh?"

Sarah would never describe Val as being in her golden years. The sixty-five-year-old widow singlehandedly ran the feed store and handled all the equipment, from a forklift to the snowplow.

"Where's Addie this mornin'? Cinnamon had a new batch of kittens she loves to show off."

"She didn't come with me."

This fell under the "everything had changed" category.

Ordinarily, Addie loved to go into town with her. They'd stop by the Sweet Shanty when they finished running errands and eat their ice cream on the swings in the park.

This time, Addie had asked if she could stay and wait for the delivery truck with Jace.

Sarah wanted to say no. The evening before had tied her into emotional knots that she was still trying to unravel.

I made a mistake, Jace had said.

Sarah didn't know how to interpret that.

Now that Addie knew Jace was her father, Sarah could no longer keep them apart. She trusted that Jace would take good care of their daughter—he had a protective streak as wide as the Wisconsin River—but sharing Addie...that would take some getting used to.

They needed to talk. After Addie had hugged Jace, Sarah hadn't known what to say. All Addie knew was that her dad had returned. For Sarah, it was way more complicated than that. Because her feelings for Jace were...complicated.

"She'll see the kittens next time," Val said cheerfully. Another wink. "And they'll be old enough to leave their mama for a new home."

More vet bills?

Sarah's smile slipped sideways. Addie would love a kitten, but there was no way they could add to the menagerie while the future was so uncertain. Sarah hoped there was enough money in the budget to pay Dr. Callahan.

"How much do I owe you?"

Val named an amount that made Sarah cringe inside. "The price will come down a bit if I keep it in stock," she added. "Saves me on shipping costs and you won't have to remember to order every month. A win-win."

Sarah wasn't sure she could make a long-term commitment, even for feed. At the moment, she wasn't sure about anything.

"I'll pay for today's supply and let you know."

"Fine by me. If you change your mind, give me a call."

"Can you bill the camp, please?"

Val looked uncomfortable now. "I'm sorry, Sarah, but store policy has changed since the last time you stopped in. I'll need the payment up front from now on."

"Oh...of course." Sarah dug out her credit card. With all the additional supplies she'd had to cover over the last few weeks, she'd have to tweak the budget until the campers began to arrive.

Val loaded the bags of feed onto another dolly and wheeled it outside. Her expression turned pensive when she spotted Maggie's SUV in the parking lot. "I sure do miss our coffee dates. Whenever I was feeling down, Maggie reminded me to look up."

"I miss her, too." What was wrong with her lately? Sarah's emotions were so close to the surface, tears threatened to spill over at the slightest disruption.

"You were like a daughter to Maggie." Val blinked rapidly. "She said so more than once. Now, make sure you bring Addie with you next time."

"I will."

Sarah's next stop was on Main Street. The corner gas station had closed when Sarah was in elementary school and a local fishing guide, Rex Ward, had bought the empty building and converted it into a bait shop.

The Hook became a popular gathering place for anyone who wanted to talk fishing and get a free cup of coffee from the bottomless pot that Rex kept on the counter. His daughter, Lindy, who'd left town after graduation, had returned out of the blue a few years ago and opened a small bookstore in the back of the bait shop. A new sign had appeared above the door. There had been rumors it wouldn't last, but The Hook and Line proved to be more popular than Rex's coffee.

Crosse Creek didn't have a library, so Lindy stocked the small space with books for all ages. It was another one of Addie's favorite stops when they were in town.

Sarah felt that familiar squeeze in her chest again.

Leaving Addie behind had left her feeling completely unmoored. Maggie had been a surrogate grandma to Addie, but with Jace, it was different. He had legal rights to their daughter.

The fears that had plagued Sarah all night washed over her again.

Would Jace demand joint custody of Addie? And if he did, what would that even look like?

It occurred to Sarah how little she knew about Jace's life, except that he was in the military. He could be deployed for months at a time, which would be difficult for Addie.

Jace would visit when it was convenient, stay long enough to disrupt their lives and then disappear again, leaving Sarah to pick up the pieces.

A bell attached to the door chimed a greeting as Sarah entered the store. The three men huddled around the coffee pot barely glanced her way. One half of the room was crowded with racks lined with hooks and fishing lures. The rest of the space held enormous metal tanks for live bait.

Sarah stepped closer to the counter but there was no sign of Rex.

"He isn't here." One of the men raised his voice over the gurgle of the aerators. He jerked his thumb at the bright yellow door that separated the bookshop from the bait store. "Lindy's in the back if you need something."

"Thank you." Sarah turned the antique knob. Even though she'd visited the bookstore dozens of times, crossing the threshold felt a little like stepping into a children's picture book.

The hardwood floors had been refinished, the bookshelves painted in alternating stripes of pale yellows, pinks, greens and soft denim blues. A circle of comfy chairs invited customers to linger. The only fish in sight were the koi swimming in the river of the colorful mural painted on the wall.

"Hey, Sarah!"

She looked over...and up.

Lindy stood on a ladder, a dustcloth in one hand and a ceramic vase in the other. Her champagne blond hair was gathered in a loose topknot. She wore baggy cotton overalls over a plain white T-shirt, and yet somehow made the ordinary ensemble look chic.

Like Sarah, Lindy had grown up in Crosse Creek. They'd attended the same schools, but Lindy had been two grades behind Sarah, with a different circle of friends and interests, so they'd never gotten to know each other very well.

"What can I do for you?" Lindy began her descent down the ladder.

"I wanted to talk to your dad about ordering bait for the first group of campers next week. We're going to need some new poles, too."

"Dad's not coming in today, but I can help you out."

"That would be great."

"No Addie today?"

Sarah pressed out a smile and shook her head.

She followed Lindy into the bait shop, saw the men had left and confessed, "The bookstore smells so much better."

Lindy laughed. "There's a reason I keep the door closed."

She pulled up the camp's file on her computer. "Other than the poles, did you want to make any changes? It looks like a standing order...pretty straightforward... Dad delivers the bait every Saturday morning through the end of summer."

"I'd like to go week by week this summer," Sarah said. "And I'll pick the order up myself, so your dad doesn't have to make a special trip out to the camp."

It probably wouldn't make a huge difference in the cost, but at this point, every little bit helped.

Lindy's lake-blue eyes met Sarah's over the counter. "I'll make a note of that," she finally said. "When does the camp open for the season?"

"Saturday." Saying it out loud made it more real.

"I'll put the order in right away." Lindy's fingers danced over the keyboard. "You said you needed poles, too?"

"Yes..." Sarah's fingers closed over the receipt from the feed store. "But those can wait. I'll take an inventory of the boat-house and see how many are salvageable."

Lindy glanced up. "Hold on a second."

She disappeared into the oversize storage closet Rex referred to as his office and emerged a few minutes later juggling an armload of fishing poles.

"Will these work?"

Sarah was a step below an amateur when it came to fishing, but even she recognized the pricey brand name on the tags.

"Companies send their newest models to fishing guides, hoping they'll show them off to their clients. Dad was just complaining the other day that they're starting to pile up back there, so he'll be thrilled I found them a good home. No charge, of course," Lindy added.

Sarah felt her cheeks heat up. "Lindy... I appreciate it, but—"

"No *buts*," Lindy said firmly. "We're helping each other. The first few months after I opened the bookstore, I think Maggie kept me in business because she'd stop by once a week and buy up half my stock."

"I didn't know that." But it would explain why the shelves in Maggie's office overflowed with books.

"At first it felt awkward. I didn't want her to think I couldn't handle things on my own, you know? One day she said that it's important to leave a legacy—but starting one takes a little help sometimes." Lindy's eyes sparkled. "And a leap of faith."

"A leap of faith," Sarah echoed.

"Like you did...taking over the camp."

Sarah blushed again.

Because the first thing that came into her mind hadn't been Four Arrows.

It was Jace.

Jace could get used to this.

Addie's chatter drowned out the music playing in the background and the birds in the trees.

She'd talked nonstop since the delivery driver had left and they'd moved onto Addie's favorite task—cleaning and polishing the tack.

"When I grow up, I want to be a veterinarian *and* start a therapy riding camp here." Addie paused to inspect a leather rein. "My friend Gina is in a wheelchair and she's always drawing pictures of horses in art class but she's never ridden one because her mom doesn't think it's safe." She looked up at Jace. "I think everyone who loves horses should have a chance to ride one, don't you?"

Jace nodded, blown away by her sweetness and sensitivity. Addie reminded him so much of Sarah. She might have claimed she was more comfortable with her four-legged friends, but her patience had extended to all the campers.

"What did you want to be when you were my age?" Addie asked.

Anyone but Jace Marshall.

The answer popped into Jace's head before he had time to think about it. His mom's two-year battle with leukemia and his dad's binge drinking had started when Jace was Addie's age. He'd made his own meals, gotten himself ready for school, spent way too many evenings and weekends alone in front of the television.

"I can't remember." There'd been so many unknowns, Jace had learned it was safer to live day by day. "I watched a lot of movies when I was eleven. The ones I liked the best were about planes."

He'd envied those pilots as the wheels left the ground, leaving everything else behind.

"Mom doesn't let me watch a lot of TV." Addie sighed. "When I looked for your address, I saw a picture of you in a helicopter."

"I joined the army after high school and trained to be a pilot."

"Is it scary?"

Jace thought of the sandstorms and fog, the jagged bolts of lightning descending from the clouds like javelins. The moments he was sure he'd see heaven instead of another sunrise.

"Sometimes." Addie's furrowed brow had him adding, "But I didn't reenlist, so I won't be flying helicopters anymore."

"You don't have to go back?"

"Nope."

A smile instantly replaced the frown. "I've never been on a plane, but I have a book about a wild horse that lives on Chincoteague Island. It would be fun to go there for Pony Penning Day."

"What's Pony Penning Day?"

Addie answered the question and then proceeded to provide a lively summary of the book she'd mentioned that was easier for Jace to grasp than the plot of *Anne of Green Gables*.

From there, the topic veered into horses in general and Jace soaked it in, asking questions when Addie paused to take a breath, but mostly enjoying the stories and filing away details to think about later.

Like why Four Arrows wasn't buzzing with volunteers this close to opening.

The camp was unique in that campers paid for the use of the setting and the activities. Groups who brought in their own counselors and support staff meant reduced overhead costs, but Maggie had always hired a waterfront and activities director, a camp cook and a head wrangler to oversee the equine camps. It helped that she'd insisted on keeping things simple, too. Camp-fires and outdoor games. Trail rides, swimming and stargazing.

God's creation is amazing enough. I don't have to try to one-up it, he'd heard her say on more than one occasion.

Maggie wasn't a control freak. She was a natural leader who knew how to delegate. But more than that, Maggie had fostered a feeling of community. Everyone who came to Four Arrows felt like they belonged. Jace had seen people show up unannounced and pitch in to help wherever they were needed.

Why weren't those people helping Sarah now?

"...I wanted to get a new saddle for my birthday, but Mom said we should wait until the 4-H tack sale at the end of the summer."

"I'll get you one."

"Really?" Addie's eyes went wide and Jace realized he'd said it out loud.

It's just that...he'd missed a lot of birthdays. Holidays. He had a lot to make up for.

All this time, Jace could have been contributing financially to Addie's care, but he had a hunch Sarah would be as reluctant to accept his money as she was his help.

They definitely needed to talk.

As relieved as Jace was that the truth was out in the open, Sarah had seemed more closed off after Addie had launched herself into his arms.

It probably hadn't helped that she'd asked to stay at the camp while Sarah ran some errands in town.

He knew how much it had cost Sarah to agree. And while he was thankful that she trusted him with Addie, Jace wanted more. He wanted Sarah to trust him, too.

"I'll talk to your mom first," Jace said. "But you'll have to pick out the saddle. I don't want to get mint chocolate chip instead of Blue Moon."

Addie grinned and Jace heard himself say, "Is there anything else you'd like?"

The cliché *rein it in* popped into his head, but was it so terrible that he wanted to spoil Addie a little?

Okay, maybe. Because Addie's brow had furrowed again.

"Do you…" She stopped and so did Jace's heart. As much fun as he'd been having with Addie this morning, he suspected she still had a lot of questions about his relationship with Sarah. "Do you mind if I call you Dad?"

Chapter Eleven

Now Jace understood why some of the guys in his unit broke down and cried when they received a text or photo of their kids. All that emotion had to go somewhere.

"No… I don't mind. Not at all." Jace didn't deserve the title, but it felt better than being awarded a medal of honor.

"Okay… Dad." Addie cocked her head and mischief filled her eyes. "You can call me Addie. Or Addison. You can't call me Addie Oakley, though. Josh Winslow calls me that and it's so annoying." She didn't look annoyed. Jace made a mental note to ask Sarah about this Winslow kid.

"Most of the time, Mom calls me Addie. Unless she's upset, then she calls me by my whole name." Addie's nose wrinkled. "It's a long one because I have two middle names. Addison Margaret Ellen Crosse."

Jace understood why Sarah had chosen Margaret. But Ellen. Ellen was his mother's name.

Sarah knew about her battle with leukemia. Before Ellen Marshall had gotten sick, she'd been a great mom. Attentive and fun. After she had died, Jace's father had refused to say her name, as if he'd blamed her for leaving them.

Had he told Sarah that, too, during one of their many conversations by the campfire?

Jace had walked out on her, yet Sarah had honored his mom, the way she'd honored Maggie, by giving their daughter her name.

He was afraid to read too much into it. He'd seen the shock on Sarah's face the day he'd arrived. She'd never expected to see him again. But had there been a moment, when she'd had Addie, that she'd hoped he would come back?

"That's a very pretty name," Jace finally said.

"Not when I was learning to spell it! It took up a whole piece of paper!"

Jace laughed. "I'm sure it did."

A vehicle rumbled down the driveway and a few seconds later, Jace heard a door slam.

"Mom's back," Addie said.

"No." Jace set down the rag and bottle of mineral oil. "It sounds like another delivery truck. I'll be right back."

Addie nodded and Jace stepped out of the barn. A half-ton pickup with a trailer was parked near the round pen. Jace spotted the driver, a middle-aged guy in dark jeans and a Western-style shirt, watching the horses vacuum up the last of their breakfast hay.

Jace's plan to fix the main gate and install a camera was going to be the next thing on his list.

"Good morning."

The guy turned in his direction and he looked a little surprised to see Jace walking toward him. "Mornin'. Sarah here?"

"Not at the moment."

"That's all right… I was in Crosse Creek and thought I'd stop by." He stretched out his hand to Autumn as the mare broke away from the herd and walked over to greet the visitors. "Decent looking bunch except for the paint over there."

Jace didn't appreciate anyone insulting Pancakes. "He's one of the best horses for beginning riders."

"What about the rest of them?" The stranger ran his hand down Autumn's withers, but to Jace, the gesture seemed more clinical than affectionate. "Are they all saddle-broke?"

"Look, Mr.—"

"Jensen. Tom Jensen."

"If you've got a son or daughter registered for equine camp and you're concerned about safety, Sarah would be better at answering your questions. She's in charge of them."

"The kids are grown up and long gone." Jensen chuckled. "My wife and I own Timber Ridge Stables and things have been going so well the past few summers, we're hoping to purchase some more horses."

Wow. Jace couldn't believe Jensen's nerve.

"Sarah isn't interested in selling any of her horses."

"Huh." Jensen whipped off his baseball cap and scratched the top of his bald head. "That's not the impression I got from the message she left on my phone."

"I'm sure you misunderstood…"

But Jensen's attention had shifted from Jace and locked on something behind them. "And how are you this morning, little lady?" he boomed.

"Good!"

Addie.

Her curiosity must have gotten the best of her, so she'd wandered out of the barn to see why Jace hadn't returned.

How to run interference? Because even if Jensen was telling the truth, Jace doubted Addie knew that her mom was thinking about reducing the herd.

He still didn't believe the guy, though. A decade ago, Jace had teased Sarah that she'd talked about the horses like they were friends. He couldn't imagine she'd be willing to part with a single one.

"Do you help your mama take care of the horses?" Jensen asked.

Addie bobbed her head. "Uh-huh."

No way was Jace going to let Jensen quiz Addie about the horses.

"I'll tell Sarah you stopped by," he said.

"She has my number." Jensen gave the herd a final sweeping glance and set his hat back on his head. Winked at Addie. "You two have a good day."

It had started out pretty great, but now Jace wasn't so sure. He watched Jensen put the truck in gear and drive away.

Addie slipped her hand into Jace's as they walked back to the barn.

He'd missed out on a lot of firsts with Addie, but he planned to cherish every single one of them now.

Addie grabbed another saddle. "What did that man want?"

"To talk to your mom about something," Jace murmured.

Addie tipped her head. "I've seen him before."

Jace was afraid she would remember where and needed a distraction. She liked to talk, so...

"You asked me a question. Do you mind if I ask you some?"

"Can we take turns?"

Oh, this kid.

"Sure." Jace smiled. "But I'll start."

We should talk.

Sarah read the text message from Jace.
She'd planned to send one to him, but he'd beaten her to it.
She typed a response.

Patio at ten o'clock. Addie will be in bed.

She hit Send and a few seconds later, a message popped up.

It's a date.

Butterflies took wing in Sarah's stomach, even though she told herself it was only a figure of speech. *Not* a real date. She and Jace would talk about their expectations. Establish sound ground rules.

Alone.

The butterflies, who obviously didn't care about expectations and ground rules, increased in number.

Sarah tried to ignore them and continued unpacking the boxes that had arrived.

Addie had attached herself to Jace after Sarah had returned from running errands, leaving her to stock the pantry shelves alone all afternoon. She'd placed the order months ago, but in past years, Jean would already be at Four Arrows, organizing the pantry and working on menus for special events.

When Jean had called, Sarah had been worried about finding someone with the same knowledge and experience to replace her. Now, she'd settle for someone who knew her way around a kitchen.

"Mom?" Addie's voice preceded her entrance into the cafeteria.

Pray Big.

The message Addie had painted on one of the rocks popped into Sarah's mind.

She prayed. Prayers that were more cautious than bold. Because she didn't believe He would answer? Or because Sarah wasn't sure He was listening anymore?

But hadn't Jesus told his disciples to be more like little children? Like Addie, who expected that a big God could do big things?

"Mom?"

"I'm in the pantry," Sarah called back.

"I told Dad about the bridge and he wants to look at it. Can I go with him?"

Dad.

Less than twenty-four hours ago, he'd been Jace.

Things were changing so rapidly, Sarah's head was having a difficult time keeping up with her heart. Right now, the latter was turning somersaults in her chest.

"Addie…did Jace tell you to call him that?"

"No, I asked him and he said it was all right." Addie searched Sarah's face and whatever she saw there stripped away her smile. "Is it all right with you, Mom?"

What could she say?

"Of course."

She and Jace definitely needed to talk.

"So, I can go with him?"

Sarah glanced at her watch. "Be back by five for supper."

"I will! Thanks!"

Sarah collapsed against the wall after Addie left.

"Okay, God," she whispered. "I'm asking. I can't run Four Arrows without a cook and a groundskeeper."

Sarah didn't expect an answer right away. She glanced at the receipt from the delivery driver and went to check the freezer to make sure the order was fulfilled.

The first thing she saw when she opened the door was a single-serving container of ice cream. Her favorite kind, of course. With a cherry-red bow on top. And a note.

Take a break.

Sarah had no idea when Jace had found the time to buy the treat, but she reached for the carton and sent up an addendum to her prayer.

"I know I just told You that I need a cook and a groundskeeper, Lord, but what am I supposed to do about Jace?"

There was no swift answer to that question, either.

Addie returned at five on the dot. Sarah expected Jace would have already been invited for supper, but Addie informed her that he had some things to do at the lodge. While Sarah grilled hot dogs for supper, Addie filled her in on every moment she'd spent with him.

"We cleaned up the tack room and Dad asked me lots of questions."

Sarah swallowed hard. "Like what?"

"What's my favorite class in school." Addie swirled a french fry through the pool of ketchup on her plate. "I told him science, and that's his favorite, too! Do you know what he wanted to be when he grew up?"

Sarah shook her head. She didn't know where Jace's desire to fly had originated.

"He watched a lot of TV when he was my age and movies about planes were his favorite."

Ellen Marshall had been sick for several years before she'd passed away. Jace had mentioned once he'd had to entertain himself while she rested.

Sarah wasn't going to feel sorry for Jace. She wasn't.

I made a mistake by not coming back.

Jace's statement was a song Sarah couldn't get out of her head. She wanted to believe him, but it didn't erase the pain of his casual dismissal of their time together. And the only reason he'd come back was because of the promise he'd made to Maggie. He hadn't come back for her.

"I told him that I have *two* middle names," Addie continued. "Margaret, because of Maggie, and Ellen." A hint of mischief danced in her eyes. "And you call me Addison Margaret Ellen Crosse when you're upset."

Jace wasn't stupid. He had to have realized Sarah had given Addie his mother's name. But would he know why?

When it was time to fill out the birth certificate, Sarah had added Ellen's name. It had seemed like a small way to remember the first woman who'd loved Jace.

Sarah had no idea how Jace would feel about it, though. He'd been reluctant to talk about his foster families, but based on the tiny bits and pieces of information that slipped out during conversation, Sarah had formed a picture of his life in the Marshall house. Jace had nothing good to say about Brad Marshall, but he'd loved his mom.

"He asked what my favorite color is." Addie popped a fry in her mouth, unaware of the memories she'd disturbed. "Who's my best friend, but I couldn't say Star."

For all that Jace didn't know about their daughter, there was a lot he'd already figured out.

"You said Maisey, didn't you?" Sarah knew her daughter, too.

"Uh-huh." Addie reached for another fry. "He asked some questions about you, too."

"Like what?" Sarah strove to keep her tone casual.

"He asked what makes you laugh."

What made her...laugh?

Why would Jace want to know that?

"What did you say?" Sarah was almost afraid to ask.

"Me."

Sarah laughed. "True."

"And if you have any friends."

Sarah suddenly lost her appetite. Jace might have a right to know more about his daughter, but he didn't have to delve into her personal life. Or lack thereof.

Sarah had had friends in high school, but most of them had moved away after graduation. The ones who'd stayed had done things the right way. Married and then started families.

After her father had left and Sarah moved to Four Arrows, Maggie had become her friend and confidante. Maggie had encouraged her to get out and do things, but Sarah had preferred to stay at home. The horses didn't gossip about her. Didn't tell her that she would be forever defined by her "mistake," like her father had.

This time, Sarah didn't want to know what Addie's response had been.

"I'll clean up. It's a shower night for you." Sarah began to gather the plates.

Addie snagged one more fry. "Jace let me ask him questions, too, so it was fair."

Sarah had a few that required an answer, too. Unlike Addie, though, she wasn't looking forward to the conversation.

Between cleanup and their nighttime routine, the rest of the evening seemed to fly by while Sarah's tension increased.

At nine thirty, Sarah checked on Addie—sound asleep—and slipped outside. In the Northwoods, summer didn't start because it said so on a calendar, but all the signs were here. The air was warm and fragrant and a half-moon played hide-and-seek in the branches of the trees.

Sarah felt Jace's presence before she saw him. And the absolutely ridiculous way her pulse spiked when he stepped into view had her rethinking her request to meet on the patio.

Suddenly, the space seemed too small. Too intimate. Especially when Jace attempted to fold his large frame into one of the chairs, failed and sat down next to her on the wicker loveseat instead.

She'd gotten used to seeing him in faded jeans and a T-shirt, but this evening he wore gray cargo pants and a cotton button-down. His hair was damp from a recent shower and some rebellious strands had started to curl a little. Sarah almost reached out to smooth them back into place...and she was in trouble.

Sarah didn't want to be attracted to him, but everything inside of her wanted to inch closer. She scooted away from him instead.

Jace didn't seem in any rush to start the conversation, so Sarah dove in.

"How does the bridge look?" Business. Business was a good place to start. "Last fall when I checked it, some of the support posts seemed loose."

"They're not only loose, they're rotting away at the base," Jace said bluntly. "Whoever built the bridge didn't use treated wood."

Sarah saw a trip to the lumberyard in her future.

"I can reroute the riding trail until it's fixed," she told him. "You don't have to worry about it." And she wouldn't have to worry about another bill.

"Sarah—"

She inwardly braced herself, expecting Jace to push back.

"Tom Jensen stopped by when you were running errands today."

This wasn't on the list of discussion points Sarah had put together in her head. She stared at Jace, speechless, as the words sank in. Dread followed.

"What did he say?"

"He was asking about the horses."

"Was Addie there?"

Jace gave her a long look. "No," he finally said. "But now I know Jensen wasn't making things up. Are you planning to sell some of the horses?"

Was that a hint of judgment in his tone? Because Sarah had been getting by without any input from him, thank you very much.

"Dr. Callahan told me the Jensens were looking for some good trail horses. I left Tom a message...asking for more information."

"Why?"

Sarah didn't want to talk about it. She started to rise to her feet, but Jace was faster. His fingers closed around her wrist. It wasn't a firm grip—she could have broken free easily— but Sarah was so shocked by the warmth of his touch that she froze in place.

"Sarah...what's going on?" Jace's eyes searched her face. "You feel the same way about those horses as Maggie felt about her books. I can't believe you'd part with a single one."

"I may not have a choice." Sarah pressed her lips together, but the damage was done.

"Talk to me," Jace urged. "Please. Did Maggie leave the camp in bad shape financially?"

"No, her mistake was leaving the camp to *me*. I don't know why she thought I could do this, Jace. When problems came up, Maggie always knew how to fix them. I don't.

"Several groups that reserved a week over a year ago canceled recently, and I haven't been able to fill the spots. The first campers arrive in less than a week. I've got my returning college students to fill in the gaps, but there's no one to oversee the kitchen and take care of the grounds. I could hire people, but that would cut into the budget. Donations have gone down since Maggie died, so I'm on shaky ground as it is. The horses…" She paused, unable to voice the truth.

"Are expensive."

"The equine camps are popular, but insurance has gone up, along with the cost of feed and veterinary bills. I have to make a decision based on reality, not…wishes and dreams."

Jace was silent, and Sarah wondered if he regretted encouraging her to talk to him. Because once she started, she couldn't stop. Or was he thinking the same thing Sarah was? That Maggie should have left Four Arrows to someone else?

"Maggie didn't make a mistake," he finally said. "She knew you loved Four Arrows as much as she did, so who better to take over when she was gone?

"And she didn't leave you alone, Sarah. The photobooks in her office are proof. There are hundreds of people whose lives were changed because of the camp."

"Because of *Maggie*," Sarah corrected. "Everyone loved and respected her. I'm the girl who got pregnant and needed a place to stay after her own father kicked her out of the house. Not exactly the kind of person who inspires confidence."

Jace's eyes darkened.

"That's not true."

"How do you know? You've been here less than two weeks."

Jace's jaw went tight.

This wasn't the way she'd expected their evening to go. Sarah thought she would be in control of the conversation. Calmly discuss the future.

Now tears clogged her throat and burned her nose, and Sarah didn't want to talk at all. She'd already said too much. Things she'd never even shared with Maggie.

That was the trouble when it came to Jace—she didn't think. The feelings he stirred inside were downright dangerous.

And what did a girl do in a dangerous situation?

If she was smart, she fled.

But Jace was smart, too. And Sarah's escape route was suddenly obstructed by an immovable object.

Chapter Twelve

Jace didn't think. He reacted.

One moment, he was standing in front of Sarah. The next, she was in his arms.

Her body stiffened, and then she melted against him. And then, a shudder ripped through her slender frame. And another. Jace could feel the moisture that soaked through the thin fabric of his shirt and drew her closer.

He didn't know what to do with a woman's tears, but he knew what to do in a storm. Hold tight. Pray.

Is that how Sarah saw herself? Did she think people were judging her based on a decision she'd made at eighteen? Because Jace didn't see her that way.

Sarah was a wonderful mother. Strong. Sweet. Brave. Sarah thought Maggie had an impact on his life, and although the camp director had been instrumental in pointing Jace to the path of faith, Sarah was the one who'd broken through his walls and made him take a risk on love.

And how had he repaid her?

By breaking her heart.

The shudders began to subside and Jace could sense Sarah's struggle to regain control.

"I'm sorry." Her voice was muffled against his chest and she moved restlessly in his arms, but Jace didn't want to let go yet.

She wasn't the only one who'd been keeping a tight lid on her emotions.

Addie was a gift he didn't deserve, but even before Jace had found out he was a father—the day he'd turned around and had seen Sarah standing in the driveway behind him—Jace realized that none of the places he'd lived had felt like home because she hadn't been there.

"I didn't mean to do that." Sarah reared back a few inches and tried to smooth the wrinkles out of his shirt. "You're all wet and I'm a mess—"

"You're beautiful," Jace said, stopping her. He brushed a damp strand of hair off her flushed cheek and tucked it behind her ear.

She ducked her head self-consciously, clearly not believing him. Jace's fingers traced a path down the curve of her cheek and lifted her chin. Tears still shimmered in her eyes, but it was the denial Jace saw that cut deep.

"Beautiful," he repeated. "Inside and out."

She caught her lip between her teeth in the nervous little habit that usually made Jace smile. Not this time. Because he didn't want her to doubt it was true.

And then he ruined it by bending his head and kissing her.

He heard Sarah's quick intake of breath, felt her hands flutter against his chest…and then slide around his waist. Her lips were satin soft beneath his as she leaned into him, kissing him back. Jace tasted salt tears and a sweetness he hadn't been able to forget.

"Sarah." He murmured her name and felt the shiver that rippled through her.

A split second later, she broke the connection and stumbled away from him.

Reality washed over Jace and he silently kicked himself for taking advantage of the moment. If he'd wanted to prove to Sarah that he'd changed, kissing her wasn't the way to go about it.

"I'm sorry." Now he was the one apologizing. "I didn't mean for that to happen."

Something flashed in Sarah's eyes before she turned away from him. She was almost to the door before Jace realized what was happening.

"Sarah? Wait."

This time, she paused and glanced over her shoulder.

"Jace... I can't do this again."

This.

Trusting him? Trusting herself?

Jace had to convince Sarah that he wasn't interested in reliving the past, either. It was the future that he cared about. Their future.

"What did you do?"

Mason answered Jace's call with a question instead of a hello.

"Why would you... Nothing, okay?" Except that kiss last night wasn't nothing. Jace hadn't been able to stop thinking about it. Regretting it.

Kind of.

Which made him a first-class jerk, right?

Except... Sarah had kissed him back.

"Hold on." Jace heard a commotion in the background. "Sorry. Snow decided she wanted to go outside and didn't care the screen door was closed. So, you didn't do anything but you're calling at...seven a.m."

"You've been up for hours." So had Jace.

He'd already hiked the three miles to Maple Hill. The place where he and Sarah had gone the night before he'd left. That night, Jace's emotions had overridden his self-control. This time, he'd had a long talk with God.

"Addie knows I'm her dad."

Mason's low whistle hummed in Jace's ear. "You told her?"

"She figured it out."

"How did she react?"

"She said she'd prayed that I would come back someday."

"Wow."

Right?

"Sarah still doesn't trust me."

"She doesn't know you. At least the *you* everyone else knows," Mason amended. "Don't get a big head, but you're the golden retriever of trustworthy."

Golden retriever? What happened to Falcon? Confident. Fearless. Laser-focused on the mission.

But the mission had changed. His confidence was shot and Sarah had turned his world inside out and upside down.

"What's the plan?" Mason asked.

"My two weeks is almost up and I don't think Sarah is going to beg me to stay. She won't ask for help, but she's burning herself out trying to keep the camp running. I have no idea what to do."

Mason laughed, which Jace thought was kind of jerky under the circumstances.

"Why is that funny?"

"I was there when you said you weren't going to reenlist because you'd been feeling a nudge that God had something else in mind for you, remember?" he said. "I hoped it meant you'd be working for me, but now you find out you have a daughter with the woman you love and—"

"Hold on," Jace interrupted. "I never said I loved Sarah."

"I'm sorry." Mason laughed again. "Did you miss something?"

Yes, he had. Sarah. For the past ten years. Jace's feelings for her hadn't died. They'd been dormant. Resurrected the first time Sarah had smiled at him.

"How I feel about Sarah doesn't change the way she feels about me," he pointed out.

"Like I said, give her time."

Time was what Jace was running out of.

"Thanks. I'll keep you posted."

"And I'll keep praying." Mason sounded serious now. "God's got you, Jace."

Jace knew that, but it was always good to be reminded.

He hung up the phone and went upstairs to make himself some breakfast. From the window, he could see Sarah's cabin. No lights on. The barn was dark, too.

Suddenly restless, Jace decided to drive to the lumberyard and pick up what he needed to fix the bridge. There were only a few cars in the parking lot, and the small cluster of employees chatting by the paint department barely glanced at Jace as he walked in.

The bridge had been in worse shape than he'd expected, but he hadn't told Sarah he planned to replace the whole thing.

"Jace?"

He turned at the sound of a voice behind him.

The guy standing in the aisle looked vaguely familiar. Craggy features, piercing blue eyes, a shock of blond hair and an easy smile.

He must have seen the confusion on Jace's face because he thrust out his hand. "Bryce Weston."

Jace hadn't recognized the face, but he recognized the name. Bryce, a seminary student, had been a fixture at the camp the summer Jace lived there. "Campfire. You led the worship time."

Bryce chuckled. "I'm flattered you remembered. Now I'm a youth pastor at Crosse Creek Community. I'm not sure if my singing has improved, but I can actually play the guitar instead of just strum it now."

Jace grinned. "Good to know."

His memory uploaded an image of the lanky guy who'd led devotions at Campfire several times over the course of the summer.

Jace had tolerated Bryce because he hadn't been one of the college guys who'd ogled Sarah, but he'd avoided him, too. Bryce had talked about a Good God, but Jace had figured that came easy to a guy who had a good life. Put him in Jace's shoes and he might have sung a different tune. No pun intended.

"So…what brings you back to Crosse Creek?"

How much time did the guy have?

Jace went with the easiest answer. "Four Arrows."

"I've met a lot of people who trace the beginning of their faith journey to the camp and end up back here for a visit."

Jace saw the question in Bryce's eyes.

Was Jace one of them?

"I didn't know about Maggie until I got here," Jace admitted. "I was heading up to a friend's place in Minnesota and decided to stop and say hello."

As far as explanations went, it sounded a little flimsy even to Jace's ears, but he wasn't going to mention Addie's postcard.

Bryce sighed. "Maggie's death hit all of us pretty hard. Sarah most of all, though."

Jace tamped down his frustration. If the youth pastor knew that, why weren't more people helping her?

As difficult as it was to believe, was there truth in what Sarah had told him? Had people shunned her because of Addie?

"She has a lot of responsibility." Jace heard the edge in his voice and Bryce must have heard it, as well, because he frowned. "That's why I'm here." He motioned to the lumber. "The bridge that connects two of the trails needs to be replaced."

"You're staying there?" Bryce didn't look so easygoing now.

Jace guessed the pastor's memory had just uploaded an image of Jace from ten years ago, too.

"Temporarily—in Maggie's apartment," Jace said. He didn't want the guy to jump to any conclusions. "I just finished my last tour—" *See? I'm one of the good guys* "—and there's a lot of work to do before the camp opens this weekend."

"I'm sure there is. The youth group used to volunteer their time, raking and cleaning up the waterfront. Maggie would have a big cookout afterward, although I'd like to think the kids helped out of the goodness of their hearts and not because she'd perfected the grilled cheeseburger." He chuckled. "I'd tease Maggie when she'd hand out chocolate chip cookies on Sunday mornings along with a sign-up sheet for volunteers. *Is this a bribe or a thank you?* She'd wink and tell me it was a little bit of both."

"Sarah's not Maggie, though."

"I realize that." Bryce studied him. "But Sarah has attended Crosse Creek Community all her life. She's part of the family. If she needs help with anything, we're there for her."

"Like I said… Sarah isn't Maggie." Jace paused. "How long has it been since she's asked?"

Understanding dawned in Bryce's eyes. "About three years."

That's what Jace had suspected.

"Wasn't Sarah the head wrangler the summer you stayed at Four Arrows?" Bryce asked slowly.

The guy had a pretty decent memory…and, judging from his narrowed gaze, a grasp of basic math.

Jace met his gaze.

"I didn't know," he said simply.

"And now that you do?"

"That's up to Sarah…but I'm praying."

"Can I help you find something?" A teenager wearing canvas overalls and a store ID badge jogged up to them.

Jace fished a scrap of paper out of his pocket. "I need everything on this list."

The kid looked at it and nodded. "If you pull your vehicle around back, I'll help you load it up."

"It was nice seeing you again." Jace managed to take two steps when Bryce caught up to him.

"Jace? What time are you starting on that bridge?"

* * *

Sarah tried to concentrate on the row of colorful bins lined up on the table in the arts and crafts cabin, but her gaze kept straying to the window. Landing on the empty spot next to the lodge that had become Jace's personal parking space.

She'd noticed his truck wasn't there when she and Addie walked down to the barn to feed the horses, but she couldn't imagine where Jace had gone so early in the morning.

Unless it hadn't been morning. Maybe he'd packed up his things and left after she'd abandoned him on the patio the night before.

After the kiss.

The kiss Jace said shouldn't have happened.

Sarah didn't know what was worse. That she'd cried in his arms or that she'd kissed him back.

Their talk had gone off-script, too. Sarah had wanted to stay in control, but when she'd found out that Tom Jensen had stopped by, all her fears about the future had rushed to the surface. And then, Jace's genuine concern about the camp had literally opened the floodgate and Sarah had been powerless to stop herself from confiding in him.

And she was looking out the window again.

Sarah yanked her gaze back to the task in front of her, making sure the ratio of feathers, beads and tiny silver charms matched the number of campers who'd be arriving for the first week of camp.

At least this area was covered. All Sarah had to do was provide the supplies and the camp counselors supervised the creative activities.

A vehicle cruised slowly past the lodge, but it was a compact car, not Jace's pickup.

"I'll be right back, Ads."

Addie, who'd discovered a box of beads and was stringing them onto a yellow satin ribbon, nodded but didn't look up.

Sarah stepped outside and saw Lindy Ward in the driver's seat. The bookstore owner spotted her, too, and pulled up next to the cabin. The window rolled down.

"Hey, Sarah! Is it okay to park here?"

Sarah nodded cautiously, not sure why Lindy had driven out to Four Arrows. She reached for her cell to see if there were any missed calls or texts and realized she'd left it at the cabin.

"Great!" Lindy cut the engine, hopped out of the vehicle and spun around in a slow circle. Sighed. "I forget how beautiful it is here. And peaceful."

Sarah felt a pinch of guilt.

Sometimes, caught up in the business of the day, she forgot, too.

"Is there a problem with my order?" she finally asked.

"Order...oh, no." Lindy smiled. "I got Pastor Bryce's email and closed up the bookstore a few hours early today."

"Email?" Sarah was still confused.

"He sent a message through the Good Neighbor Line at church, asking if anyone could spend a few hours helping you get the camp ready for opening day."

"How did..."

The rest of the sentence trailed off as a procession of vehicles, led by the vintage VW van that transported the church youth group from place to place, rattled down the driveway. The moment it rolled to a stop, the doors popped open and released an avalanche of teenagers. Bryce appeared a few seconds later, dressed in work clothes and a pair of well-worn hiking boots.

He spotted Sarah and Lindy and strode over.

"Hey, Sarah!" he greeted her cheerfully. "I ran into Jace at the hardware store and he mentioned you had a bridge that needed replacing. The kids have been looking for something to do now that school is out, so I thought you might be able to use a few extra hands while they burned off some energy.

"While I was making calls, I realized there might be some

other last-minute projects, so I cast a wider net, so to speak." He grinned at Lindy. "No pun intended."

"Dad runs a bait shop." Lindy's eyes rolled toward the sky. "I'm used to it. He's the king of fishing jokes."

Sarah was trying to process everything the pastor had said but couldn't get past the *I ran into Jace.*

Maggie had hired Bryce, a seminary student, several summers in a row to lead worship at Campfire in the evenings. Bryce had fallen in love with Aimee, one of the local volunteers, so no one had been surprised when he'd applied and been hired by Crosse Creek Community after graduation.

Because sometimes a couple got their happily-ever-after.

She shook the thought aside as Bryce continued. "Me and some of the guys will help Jace, and Scott can supervise another group. Tell us what you need done and we'll divide and conquer."

Sarah scanned the group of volunteers who'd drifted down to the waterfront. In addition to the teens, Scott and his wife, Hannah, who served on the worship team, she counted half the members of the adult singles group. A quick head count told Sarah there were more than "a few extra hands." In one afternoon, this many volunteers could cut Sarah's to-do list in half.

"Thank you," she murmured. "I really appreciate this, Bryce."

"I get to spend the afternoon outside instead of in my office." Bryce flashed the warm smile that had earned the trust of dozens of teens. "I should be thanking you. Now, I'll get my crew together and we'll get to work!"

He jogged back to the group of teens, pausing to wave at a familiar pickup truck that had pulled into the empty space Sarah had been watching all morning. A moment later, Jace swung down from the driver's seat.

She couldn't recall a time that Jace and Bryce had spoken to each other that summer, and now the two men clasped hands and grinned at each other like they were the best of friends.

Why did Jace feel so obligated to help her?

Out of guilt? Did he feel sorry for her?

And why had he kissed her?

Thinking about that kiss turned Sarah's knees to liquid again.

"Um…" Lindy cleared her throat.

Because Sarah had forgotten she was there.

"Sorry. It's just… I can't believe he… I mean, all of you, are here."

"Power tools are beyond my skill set and I'm kind of afraid of horses, but I am fairly decent with a paintbrush."

Paint.

Right.

Get a grip, Sarah.

"I was restocking supplies in the arts and crafts area, if you'd like to help with that?"

"Let's go."

Lindy followed Sarah into the cabin and Addie's eyes lit up. "Miss Lindy! What are you doing here?"

"Your mom is going to put me to work while Pastor Bryce and his crew fix the bridge."

Addie's chair scraped against the floor. "Can I help?"

"I think we'll leave that project to the older kids."

Addie looked disappointed, but quickly recovered when Lindy admired her bracelet.

Addie had noticed Jace's absence, too. But unlike Sarah, she hadn't spent the entire morning wondering if he'd return.

Lindy opened a cabinet, pulled out a plastic storage bin and peeled off the top. "This looks like clothing."

Sarah glanced over her shoulder. "Donations and a few items from the lost and found that were never claimed. We keep them for talent night."

"Someone brought this to camp?" Lindy drew out a pink feather boa and draped it around Addie's shoulders, earning a giggle.

"Mom was in the talent show," Addie informed her. "She sang a song."

"Lip-synched," Sarah corrected with a shudder.

"That sounds like fun. At the music camp I attended, we had to audition for the final recital of the summer."

Music camp? Final recital?

Sarah realized there was a lot she didn't know about Lindy Ward.

"Mom!" Addie was looking out the window. "Dad's back! Can I show him the bracelet I made?"

Addie didn't wait for Sarah's answer. She was on her feet and out the door. It snapped shut behind her, leaving a deafening silence.

Lindy was looking out the window now, too.

The only person in sight was Jace, unloading an armload of lumber from the back of his truck.

This was something she hadn't anticipated when she hadn't discouraged Addie from referring to Jace as her dad. Sarah had attended Crosse Creek Community for years. Everyone knew she was a single mom but other than Maggie and Sarah's father, no one knew who Addie's father was.

Members of the Crosse family handled their own problems. It had been her father's mantra while Sarah was growing up.

She finally dared a look at Lindy.

"It's…complicated," she said.

"You don't owe me an explanation." Lindy reached out and squeezed Sarah's hand. "But if you ever need someone to talk to, I…I understand complicated."

All Sarah could manage was a nod, but the mixture of pain and compassion in Lindy's eyes let Sarah know that she was telling the truth.

"He liked it!" Addie returned, breathless and smiling. She plunked down at the table again and began sifting through one of the containers. "And he said I should make one for you, so I'm looking for the right charm."

"The right charm?" Sarah repeated.

"The one he said you'd like."

Sarah wondered what Jace would think that was. A horse? An arrow? An ice cream sundae?

"Found it!" Addie held up the tiny silver charm shaped like a sun.

Miss Sunshine and Blue Skies.

Sarah laughed and then she remembered something else Addie had said.

He wanted to know what makes you laugh.

Her heart stumbled.

Complicated didn't begin to describe her feelings for Jace.

Chapter Thirteen

A cheer went up when Jace set the last board in place.

"Can we eat now?" one of the teenagers asked. "I'm starving."

"You're always starving," another kid shot back good-naturedly.

Suddenly, Jace remembered what Bryce had said about Maggie hosting a cookout at the end of the work day.

He hadn't seen Sarah all afternoon, so he had no idea how she felt about the small army who'd shown up unannounced. Jace had expected Bryce to round up a couple of teenagers, but he'd taken it a step further and sent a message to the entire congregation.

According to the pastor, twenty people had responded. While their group repaired the bridge, Sarah was going to assign jobs to the rest of the volunteers.

While Bryce helped Jace load the tools and extra lumber in the cart behind the ATV, it occurred to him that Sarah didn't know some of them expected to be fed at the end of the day.

The sight that greeted Jace as his crew returned to the lodge stopped him in his tracks.

The shoreline had been raked smooth and orange life jackets hung in neat rows on the side of the boathouse. A line of women, led by Sarah, were transporting kayaks from an outbuilding to a row of wooden racks near the water.

She was smiling, so that was a good sign.

The groups met at the edge of the lake and Bryce's teens immediately discarded their shoes and waded in, splashing and chasing each other through the shallow water like puppies.

Bryce groaned. "Sorry. I should have seen that coming. Fortunately, boys air-dry fairly quickly and I always keep some towels in the van. I'll be right back."

"We'll get the last of the kayaks, Sarah," a woman with bleach-blond hair said.

The rest of the women followed, leaving Sarah behind.

"Where's Addie?"

"Hannah's daughters came along, so Addie took them to the barn. I'm guessing Star is getting another spa day." Sarah kept her gaze trained on the boys. "Did you ask Bryce to organize this?"

The moment of truth.

"We ran into each other in the lumber section of the hardware store. I mentioned that I was replacing the bridge here."

Now she turned to look at him, and Jace braced himself. There was a good chance that orchestrating a bunch of volunteers to descend upon the camp would be considered "swooping."

"Thank you."

Jace blinked. Sarah always took him by surprise.

"Don't thank me yet." Time to fess up. "I think you're expected to feed them now."

"Feed them?" Sarah echoed.

"Bryce mentioned that Maggie hosted a cookout whenever there was a volunteer workday. Apparently, her cheeseburgers were legendary."

Sarah wasn't listening anymore. She was taking a silent head count and, if possible, her eyes got bigger as the tally increased.

Strike four? Or five?

Jace was losing track.

"They'll understand if you aren't prepared to provide dinner," he said. "It's a lot of extra work—"

"You can fly helicopters, but do you know how to grill?"

Jace had cooked over an open fire on more than one occasion. That had to count.

"Yes?"

"I don't know Maggie's secret burger recipe, but if there's enough cheese, no one will notice. The delivery driver should have left premade patties, but I didn't get a chance to unpack all the boxes."

"I signed for it," Jace said. "We've got chips. Rice. Canned vegetables. Twelve bottles of ketchup."

"We can work with that. The grills are still in the storage shed, but it's time to bring them out anyway."

We.

Jace liked the sound of that, even if the only reason Sarah had included him was because he was the one who'd inadvertently put her in charge of feeding the multitude.

By the time he and Bryce had set up the grills, Sarah and a petite blonde named Lindy had the preparations well underway.

When Bryce offered to make the burgers, Sarah waved him away with the spatula. "Thank you, but Jace is going to help me with the grilling."

Jace wrestled down a smile of his own. Sarah might think this was a punishment, but if it meant working alongside her, he was more than willing. He loved the way her teeth skimmed over her lower lip when she was concentrating. Loved how she could perform a multitude of tasks at once, yet knew Addie's exact location. Loved the color that bloomed in her cheeks whenever their eyes met—which made him wonder if she was thinking about that kiss, too…

Okay. Yes. He loved *her*.

The guys in Jace's unit had loved giving him a hard time. Claimed that his only long-term relationship was with his helo.

Jace had shrugged off the teasing comments. He'd made a commitment when he'd signed on with the military. There hadn't been time for romance. Now he wondered if it was because a green-eyed girl had staked her claim on his heart and there hadn't been room for anyone else.

Bryce sidled up to the grill and eyed the steaming burgers Sarah had stacked on the platter. "Everything looks delicious."

She laughed. "That's because you're hungry."

Jace loved hearing her laugh, too.

A line formed next to the grill and Bryce held up his hand. "I'd like to give thanks before we start." He waited until everyone was quiet before bowing his head. "God, thank You for bringing us together. For the beauty of Your creation and providing for our needs. Thank You for this food and the hands that prepared it."

A chorus of *amens* followed the prayer.

Jace filled his plate and scanned the picnic tables. Sarah was sitting next to Lindy, but there was an empty space next to her.

Jace hesitated. She might have enlisted his help to flip burgers, but that didn't mean he'd earned the right to sit next to her.

Not only that, he'd been working on the bridge the majority of the day, so no one had paid much attention to him. Now Jace felt the weight of every curious glance cast his way.

Crosse Creek was a small town; the congregation that attended Sarah's church even smaller. The volunteers would be wondering who Jace was and why he was at the camp.

Jace was working on an exit plan when Bryce stood up and waved.

"Jace...over here."

He made his way to the table and the teens shifted to make room. Half of them played on the high school football team and were already in the middle of a heated discussion about the upcoming season, so no one paid any attention to Jace. No curious glances. No questions. Just a "Please, pass the ketchup" once in a while.

Jace slid a speculative look at Bryce. The pastor intercepted it with an innocent smile that didn't fool Jace at all. He'd have to remember he wasn't the only one gifted in strategy.

"Who's ready for dessert?"

Dessert?

Jace twisted around just in time to see Sarah emerge from the cafeteria with a tray of ice cream bars that had been temporarily stored in the walk-in freezer until they were transported to the General Store.

Jace had seen the receipt when he'd signed for the order. It wasn't simply dessert. It was a generous gift on Sarah's part.

"Ms. Crosse?" The burly kid next to Jace had finished off the frozen treat in two bites. "Can we have a campfire?"

Everyone turned toward Sarah to see what her response would be.

Jace wanted to intervene, remind them that she'd already created a whole dinner out of a few loaves and fishes, or, in their case, a box of frozen hamburger patties, coleslaw and baked beans, but Sarah was already nodding her agreement.

In record time, wooden benches and chairs were rounded up and arranged around the firepit.

"Too bad I didn't bring my guitar," Bryce joked as everyone found a place to sit.

The laughter and conversation quieted as the crackle of the fire grew louder and one of the women exhaled a long breath.

"Oh, this brings back memories. My parents sent me here for a week every summer when I was growing up, and I loved every minute of it. Capture the flag. Kayak races."

"S'mores," someone else piped up.

"Overnight campouts on horseback."

"Hiking."

Jace glanced at Sarah. She sat in an Adirondack chair, Addie cocooned in a fleece blanket beside her. Sarah's ponytail was a little askew and the firelight ignited a hint of copper in the wisps that had escaped, but it was impossible to tell what she was thinking.

How did it feel to hear people sharing their favorite memories? A long time ago, Four Arrows might have been the highlight of her summer. Now it was home. A home she could lose if things didn't turn around.

"Midnight volleyball," the man sitting next to Pastor Bryce added.

The teenagers suddenly stirred to life and leaned forward to look at him more closely.

"Midnight volleyball? What's that?" one of them demanded.

The man looked a little sheepish when his wife speared him with a look. It was too late, though. He'd already gotten everyone's attention.

"Some of us would sneak out after curfew to play," he finally admitted. "Maggie caught us one night and we got kitchen duty for breaking the rules. The next day, she handed us a volleyball wrapped in glow-in-the-dark tape and added Midnight Volleyball to the list of the activities."

"Hey," the guy sitting next to him protested. "How come we never knew about that?"

The flash of a grin. "It was only for senior high."

The teens immediately turned to Bryce. "Can we do that?"

"Sorry." Bryce tempered his answer with a smile. "It's been a long day and your parents are picking you up in—" he glanced at his watch "—fifteen minutes, so it's time I get you back to the church."

A chorus of groans followed his announcement, but Jace was relieved the youth pastor hadn't given in. Addie's eyes were drooping and he caught Sarah stifling a yawn.

He knew she'd be awake a few more hours, checking on the horses, cleaning up the kitchen, tucking Addie into bed.

Jace was the one who'd gotten her into this, so the least he could do was help her out.

He slipped away while the volunteers reluctantly gathered up their things and drifted toward the parking lot.

Jace smiled.

This was one of *his* favorite memories.

Sarah, sitting alone by the fire after the logs had turned to embers, and everyone else had returned to their cabins. Waiting for him.

Maggie would have put him on kitchen duty if she'd known how often—and how long—they'd lingered there, talking for hours.

Jace had never opened up to anyone the way he'd opened up to Sarah. He'd told her a little about his past, but instead of judging his behavior, Sarah had encouraged him to focus on the future instead. She was the first person who'd actually believed that Jace didn't have to walk the same path his father had taken.

And what had he done to repay her belief in him?

He'd left.

Chapter Fourteen

Sarah picked up a stray blanket that had slipped underneath the bench, draped it over her arm, and scanned the area, looking for other items that may have been left behind.

"Can I stay up a little longer, Mom?" Addie punctuated the question with a yawn and Sarah laughed.

"I think you already have," she teased. "Go get ready for bed. I'll be there soon."

Another yawn. "Okay."

Lindy cast a longing glance at the fire before turning to Sarah. "I'll be back," she promised. "In fact, I might deliver your order myself and stick around for a while. Today was so much fun."

It had been fun. When Pastor Bryce arrived with reinforcements, Sarah's first impulse was to send them away with a smile. Pretend she had everything under control. But the volunteers had been so enthusiastic, she hadn't had the heart to do it. As the afternoon wore on, the work no longer felt like work. The women's laughter and lively conversation filled the gaps in Sarah's soul she hadn't realized were there.

"I'd like that," Sarah said.

Lindy smiled and headed toward the parking lot.

"I agree with Lindy."

Sarah whirled around. Mary Bellevue, the owner of the antique shop in town, stood less than a foot away. But what startled Sarah even more was when the woman reeled her in for a quick hug.

"Today *was* fun," she declared.

"But…you spent the day raking the beach."

"And loved every minute of it." Mary released her with a smile. "It's been a few years since I've been out here, but Four Arrows means a lot to me."

"You were one of the campers?"

"Not me. My niece, Rebecca Johnson."

"I remember her." An image of the slender, dark-haired girl flashed in Sarah's mind. "She was visiting for the summer and signed up for the riding camp."

"Rebecca was being bullied at school, so her parents thought a change of scenery might be good for her." Mary's smile faded a little. "I could barely get her to talk, but she loved animals. I saw a flyer for the riding program and signed her up, hoping she'd make some friends her age."

Sarah remembered Rebecca as a quiet girl who'd shied away from conversation with the other girls. But she'd instantly bonded with Marigold, a gentle palomino, and had shown a natural aptitude for riding, which Sarah had used to draw her out. By the end of camp, Rebecca had volunteered to choreograph a special equine performance to music at the talent show.

"Working with the horses gave Rebecca confidence and she joined a drill team after she went home," Mary continued. "She has a shelf filled with trophies and works for a dude ranch in Montana now."

"I'm so glad she continued her riding lessons."

"Two weeks at Four Arrows changed her life."

"Maggie had a knack for that."

"She only met Maggie once. *You* were the one that Rebecca couldn't stop talking about."

"But…all I did was teach her how to ride a horse," Sarah protested.

"You spent time with Rebecca. Listened to what she couldn't say out loud. Cheered her on."

Sarah had tried to do that with all the campers, but she'd felt an instant connection with Rebecca. Maybe because Jace had made her sensitive to the outsiders. The ones searching for a place to belong.

"The next time I talk to Rebecca, I'll tell her that I saw you. She was thrilled when I told her that you're running the camp now."

"Be sure to mention that Marigold is still here, too."

"I will."

Sarah watched the woman bustle away and reached for the blanket Addie had forgotten to take back to the cabin.

The fire was a slow simmer of embers now and Sarah resisted the urge to toss another log on it.

Jace had disappeared before the teens finished putting away the extra chairs, but did he plan to come back again?

Another memory surfaced.

She and Jace had been sitting by the fire when he'd kissed her for the first time.

Sarah had turned out the horses and had made sure the tack was put away after a sunset trail ride with the campers when she'd found a note taped to Autumn's stall.

I saved you a s'more.

They'd competed in archery, talked about anything and everything as they walked the trails together, but Sarah had always been the one to seek him out.

She'd found Jace alone by the firepit and his slow smile, the warmth in his eyes, told Sarah that something had changed.

Sarah had sat down, feeling self-conscious and then mortified when Jace reached out and plucked a piece of straw from her hair.

She'd vaulted to her feet, wishing she'd taken the time to change out of her riding clothes. Or brush her hair.

But she'd been too eager to see Jace.

He'd blocked her path that night, too.

"I'm a mess," she'd mumbled.

"No." Jace had reached for her again, but not to pick another piece of straw from her hair.

He'd traced the curve of her cheek and tipped her face until she had no choice but to look at him. And then he'd kissed her.

It wasn't Sarah's first kiss, but it was the only one that counted. The one she'd thought about for weeks, months, after Jace left, because that was the night she'd dared to dream they had a future together.

Six weeks later, Sarah found out it hadn't meant anything to him.

His kiss still had the power to turn her inside out, but she was no longer a naive teenager.

She wasn't sure about the future, either. But one thing she did know? It was a promise to Maggie that had kept Jace at Four Arrows. Once that promise was fulfilled, he would leave.

Sarah tore her gaze away from the fire and bent down to retrieve a log that had rolled off the pile. She stumbled over the uneven ground and a hand came out to steady her.

"Maybe you should spray the grass with glow-in-the-dark paint."

Pastor Bryce.

Sarah chuckled. "Maybe I should."

"We're ready to roll," the youth pastor said. "I had to take a head count to make sure none of the kids were planning a game of Midnight Volleyball."

"Thank you again for coming out today."

"Like I said, I should be thanking you," Bryce said easily. "And speaking of Midnight Volleyball... I've been thinking of doing some team-building activities this summer, but it didn't occur to me that we have the perfect place a few miles down the road from the church. I'm sure you're booked through the summer, but is there a weekend or two open after your busy season? We don't need overnight accommodations since the kids live close."

"Actually…there were some cancellations." Sarah told Bryce the dates and his eyes went wide.

"Three weeks. That's even better. I'll take two of them."

"You…" Sarah must have misunderstood. "You want to reserve two weeks?"

"There's not a lot going on in a town the size of Crosse Creek," Bryce said. "I'll talk to the head of the children's ministry, too. The teens could take one week and our elementary grades the other."

"If you don't need cabins, I can give you a special day rate, lunch included," Sarah offered.

"Again…great." Bryce gave her a rueful smile. "You'd think after all these years of walking with the Lord, I'd remember that He goes before me and He has my back. That's the Bryce Weston paraphrase of course, but I love how patient God is when I tend to forget."

The van's headlights began to flash and he laughed. "That's my cue. I'll call you so we can figure out the details, but put us on your calendar. I don't want anyone else to take those spots."

"I will," Sarah promised.

Bryce looked thoughtful. "Hearing all the stories tonight, it reminded me how God has used Four Arrows over the years."

"I want to continue Maggie's legacy," Sarah murmured.

"Maggie's legacy isn't a place, it's caring for people, and you do that very well, Sarah Crosse." Bryce caught her gaze and held it. "But if it ever becomes difficult, don't forget that it wasn't volunteers who showed up today. It was your family. We love you and Addie and we want to be there for you."

Tears scalded Sarah's eyes.

She'd felt so alone after Maggie had died. But had it been a self-imposed exile while she'd tried to prove her worth? Prove that Maggie hadn't made a mistake when she'd left the camp to Sarah?

"Now, I better go before the parents start calling, wondering where their kids are." Bryce jogged toward the van, leaving Sarah alone by the fire to absorb everything that had just happened.

She'd made at least a dozen phone calls, trying to fill those empty weeks, and Bryce wanted to reserve two of them.

Thank You, God.

It would ease the financial burden a little, maybe enough to put off making a decision about the horses for a while.

Thinking about the horses propelled Sarah toward the barn. Addie had fed Pancakes, but she'd been putting him in the stall with some extra feed at night.

She glanced at the cabin just in time to see Addie's bedroom light go off. Fresh air, running around the camp and the warmth of the campfire had tuckered her daughter out.

Sarah had almost reached the barn when the door opened and Jace stepped out.

They'd worked side by side, making dinner for the volunteers, but suddenly, she couldn't look him in the eye.

"I put Pancakes in his stall." Jace broke the silence. "He was actually waiting for me outside the door. I think he's figured out when the sun goes down, there's an extra treat waiting for him."

Those tasks had been next on Sarah's list before she turned in for the night.

And the majority of the ones on tomorrow's list had already been taken care of. Thanks to Jace.

"Did you also use bribery to get Pastor Bryce and the youth group out here today?"

"Bribery?" Jace was the picture of innocence. "All I did was mention that I was replacing the bridge. What he did with the intel was out of my hands."

Intel?

Sarah realized she was smiling.

"I figured you still had to tuck in Addie, so I also cleaned the grills and straightened up the kitchen," Jace added.

She didn't want him to be so nice. Didn't want to…need him. But the breeze carried a hint of woodsmoke and there were a lot of things they needed to talk about.

And maybe…she wasn't ready to say good-night yet.

Sarah glanced at the fire. The pieces of kindling she'd tossed onto the embers had ignited and flames danced in the circle of stones.

"We didn't get to finish our conversation last night." Sarah hoped the darkness would hide the flare of heat in her cheeks. They both knew what had cut the evening short. "I'm sure Addie's sound asleep, so we could now. If you want to. The fire is still going."

Jace was quiet for a moment.

"I don't think that's a good idea," he finally said. "At least not tonight."

Jace's voice was soft, but Sarah felt the sting of his rejection anyway.

All it had taken was a few thoughtful gestures that Jace would have done for anyone and the walls around her heart had started to crumble. Hadn't the past taught her anything?

"All right." She stumbled backward. "I'll see you in the morning, then."

Jace blew out a sigh. "We do need to talk. But…that isn't the only thing I want to do, so it's better if we postpone our conversation until tomorrow."

Sarah stared at him and then…oh.

All she could do was nod.

Jace reached for her hand and Sarah felt the warm press of his fingers before he released her again.

"'Night, Sarah."

She watched him stride toward the lodge and disappear inside.

From the day she'd met Jace, attraction had sparked between

them. There was no denying it. For Sarah, it had deepened from awareness to love over the course of the summer, but Jace had made it clear he hadn't felt the same way.

She hadn't been enough for him then, so why would that change now? Sarah was still the same person.

There was Addie to consider, though. She'd embraced having a father without hesitation, so Sarah would have to make room in her life for Jace.

Only now, she was no longer afraid he'd work his way into her heart again.

No. Sarah was afraid it had already happened.

Jace nailed the last of the loose shingles in place.

Only a hundred or so projects left and twenty-four hours to cross them off the list.

When he'd arrived, two weeks had seemed like plenty of time to help Sarah get the camp ready to open. Now he wanted more.

A lot more.

Mason had been more than patient, but he was counting on Jace joining the next group on an upcoming backpacking trip.

"Jace?"

He almost dropped the nail gun at the sound of Sarah's voice. She stood at the foot of the ladder, looking up at him, and once again, Jace's heart imitated the *thump thump thump* of the helo's rotary blades.

She'd been getting the flower beds ready for planting all morning. Her hair was pulled back in a ponytail, her cheeks kissed pink from the sun and dirt clung to the knees of her faded jeans, but she still took his breath away.

Was he about to be scolded for tackling a project that wasn't on Sarah's to-do list? He'd seen the damage from the leak Addie had mentioned and climbed up on the roof to take a look. What he'd seen wasn't pretty. The lodge would need a new roof in a few years, but in the meantime, Jace hoped that replacing some of the shingles would prevent more damage.

"You shouldn't have any more leaks." He pressed on the shingle with the toe of his hiking boot. "I found a pallet of shingles in the shed—"

"Have you seen Addie?" Sarah cut Jace off before he could finish the sentence.

"About an hour ago. Why?"

"She asked if she could get Star and bring her back to the barn, but I just checked and she's not there. I thought maybe she was with you…or in the lodge."

Jace shook his head. With a bird's-eye view from the roof, he would have noticed if Addie had gone into the building.

"Maybe she changed her mind and went for a ride first?"

"The only thing missing from the tack room is Star's lead rope and Addie knows she can't ride bareback alone."

Okay. Now Jace was concerned.

He descended the ladder, unbuckled his tool belt and tossed it aside.

"Where would Star be this time of day?"

"The pond." Sarah must have seen something in his expression because her eyes darkened. "But it's off-limits for swimming unless I'm with her."

Off-limits, but tempting on a hot summer day.

Jace yanked his thoughts back in line. Addie wasn't a rule-breaker, like he was at that age. She'd probably lost track of the time, hanging out with her four-legged friends.

"Is Maisey with her?"

"I left her in the cabin because she likes to help me dig up the flower beds."

Jace's pulse ramped up another notch. The border collie was a natural guardian, so if Addie ran into trouble, Jace had no doubt Maisey would have sounded an alarm.

"What's the quickest way to get there?"

"The service road, but you'd still have to walk a quarter mile."

Jace visualized the trail system. Addie had specific boundaries and they'd cover more ground if they separated. "You ride Autumn and I'll take the ATV. I'm sure she's fine, though. Addie's a smart kid and like you said, she knows the rules."

Was he trying to reassure Sarah? Or himself?

Sarah nodded and jogged toward the barn while Jace headed toward the storage shed.

The key was in the ignition but when Jace turned it, the only thing he heard was an ominous click.

"Come on." He tried again. Like a temperamental actor, the ATV's engine coughed a little and then decided to play dead.

Jace didn't have time to deal with this right now.

He was working on an alternate plan when a shadow fell across him. Sarah stood in the doorway and relief poured through Jace.

"You found her?"

"I whistled for Autumn but there's no sign of her."

Sarah didn't have to tell him that was unusual, too. The mare was more devoted to Sarah than the herd and never ventured far from the barn during the day.

"If Addie's walking Star from the pond to the barn, she'll take the North trail most of the way back, right?" An image of the lightning tree flashed in his mind.

The day Addie had shown it to him, Jace had wanted to take Sarah's chain saw and cut the thing down. At her age, he would have climbed the tree every chance he got.

"She should." The tremor in Sarah's voice told Jace that her thoughts had gone that direction, too.

The property surrounding the camp had been Addie's playground since she was old enough to explore, but suddenly, all the potential dangers made Jace's gut clench.

"Then we'll start there." He touched Sarah's shoulder and she flinched. "Hey. We'll find her. She's probably on her way back already and will tease us for sending out a search party."

He forced a smile. "The ATV is acting up, so it looks like we'll both be walking."

But that didn't mean Jace was going to set a leisurely pace.

Sarah changed the original plan and stayed with him. Every bend in the trail they rounded, every straight stretch lined with trees, Jace expected to see Addie and Star.

When he made a quick detour to check the lightning tree, Sarah's strangled breath cut straight to his core, told Jace it hadn't occurred to her that Addie might have climbed the tree.

God…

It was all Jace could manage as he made his way to one of Addie's favorite spots.

His instant relief that she wasn't there combined with the fear churning in his gut pushed him into a sprint as he made his way back to Sarah.

Addie had asked if flying helicopters was scary. Not knowing where your child was was a hundred—no, a gazillion—times more terrifying.

Sarah started toward him, a question in her eyes, and Jace shook his head.

Farther down, the trees thinned and Jace caught a glimpse of the pond in the distance. Sarah picked up the pace and passed Jace as the trail narrowed.

He must really be a dad because he was already rehearsing the lecture he was going to give Addie about the importance of sticking to the plan when the pond came into view.

His gaze swept over the horses peacefully grazing beside it.

Jace had been so sure they'd find Addie here, it took a moment for his brain to process that his daughter and Star were nowhere in sight.

Sarah had noticed something else.

"Autumn…"

Jace saw her expression and took a quick head count.

Sarah's mare was missing, too.

She stumbled forward, shouting Addie's name.

Chapter Fifteen

"Sarah...wait." Jace called out to her, but Sarah didn't want to wait. She wanted to find her daughter.

A dozen possible scenarios ricocheted through her mind, feeding the fear that had taken root when Jace had veered off the trail toward the lightning tree.

Even if Addie had taken another trail back to the barn, their paths would have crossed at some point.

Jace pointed to the tree line beyond the pond. "There's a path over there. Where does it go?"

Sarah followed the direction of his gaze. "It's a deer trail. They know where the pond is, too. Addie wouldn't take Star on it, though. It's too rough and she knows she has to stay on the main trails."

Jace was already striding in that direction.

"Jace—"

He tossed a look over his shoulder.

"Whistle."

Sarah wasn't sure she could. She put two fingers between her lips and gave it her best try, though.

Her knees almost buckled when a red roan appeared in the opening between the trees a few seconds later.

Sarah broke into a run but so had Jace. Autumn tap-danced nervously as they approached, her eyes rolling back. Sarah took hold of her halter.

"Easy, girl," Sarah whispered.

Autumn calmed while Sarah's pulse accelerated to the point that she thought her heart was going to jump out of her chest.

"It's okay." She pointed to the pond and gave Autumn's flank a pat. "Go on."

Jace was already starting down the rutted path.

Sarah followed, dodging roots protruding from the ground, as she called Addie's name.

Jace stopped so abruptly that Sarah almost bumped into him.

"What…" Sarah peered around Jace and her knees almost buckled.

Addie was sprawled on the ground, almost nose to nose with the horse lying on its side.

"Addie!"

Her daughter rolled to her knees and the mare struggled to rise.

"Mom…stop. You're scaring her." Panic thinned Addie's voice. "Don't come any closer."

Sarah would have ignored the warning if Jace hadn't grasped her arm.

"Wait."

Wait? When Addie might be injured?

Sarah would have ignored him, too, but he was pointing to Star.

Bile rose in Sarah's throat.

Part of Star's torso and her back legs were wrapped in barbed wire.

"I—" Addie gulped a breath. "I couldn't leave her."

"We know." Jace sounded calm. "Are you hurt?"

"No. I saw a fawn run down the trail and I followed it. I didn't know Star was behind me…she got spooked when the mom charged us. I tried to stop her, but she jumped over the fence." Tears streamed down Addie's face. "She's bleeding…"

"It's okay." Jace took a step forward, his gaze trained on the mare now. "Just keep talking to Star."

Sarah swallowed hard. Multiple cuts, some of them deep, marked Star's legs and side. On closer examination, she could see shards of wood attached to the wire that held the horse captive. Pieces of a fence as old as the property.

Dr. Callahan was one of the first numbers in Sarah's contact list, but she'd left her cell phone in the cabin while she weeded the flowerbeds. Not that it would do any good. Reception was spotty at best this far from the lodge.

How were they going to free the horse without causing more injury?

Jace approached slowly, murmuring words of encouragement to Star and Addie. As he knelt down, he reached into the pocket of his jeans and pulled out a small but serious-looking utility knife.

Jace glanced over his shoulder and winked at her.

"Never leave home without it."

He was trying to encourage her, too.

Wild-eyed, Star's breath came out in short bursts as Jace gave her flank a soothing pat.

Sarah inched closer and reached out her hand to Addie, who grasped it so tightly that pain shot up Sarah's arm. She sank down on the ground beside her daughter and they sat without moving as the minutes ticked by.

Jace snipped at the wire, pausing whenever Star tried to roll to her feet. Sweat glistened on his brow but he remained focused, his touch gentle but sure as he worked to free Star.

Sarah realized that was only step one.

Star could have been hurt badly when she fell. Sarah had a rudimentary knowledge of how to treat minor injuries, but if there were torn muscles or fractures, even getting the horse back to the barn would pose a challenge.

One of the wooden posts dropped to the ground and Star began to thrash again, spraying her and Addie with dirt.

"Almost done, girl," Sarah whispered, praying it was true.

What would she have done without Jace?

She watched as he carefully unwrapped another piece of wire holding Star captive and paused to rub the horse's nose.

Sarah had seen Jace's patience on display since the day he'd arrived. The way he focused on a task. At eighteen, Jace had rebelled against authority; now he exuded it. She'd been shocked to find out he'd joined the military, but Sarah realized it was a good fit for a boy who'd not only wanted to prove himself, but to accomplish what God had hardwired him to do. Protect anything—or anyone—entrusted to his care.

"Addie?" Jace's voice was low, even. "I'm about to cut the last wire. When I do, Star is going to sense she's free and she's going to want to get up. I need you to move away from her, okay?"

"I don't want to," Addie said tremulously.

"I know, but we need to give Star some space." He glanced at Sarah and she could read his thoughts.

Even a horse with as sweet a temperament as Star could buck or kick—or bolt—if it was in pain.

"Trust me?"

Jace was speaking to Addie now, but the simple question cut deep. Because trust wasn't simple. Not for Sarah.

If you didn't trust anyone, they couldn't disappoint you. Reject you.

Sarah hadn't been very good at trusting God, either.

Bryce had reminded her that He was always at work, but it had been easier—no, *safer*—for Sarah to try to do it all.

"It's okay, Star," Addie whispered. "You're going to be fine. Me and Mom and Dad are right here."

Star shuddered as Addie stopped stroking her withers and scooted backward. Sarah's cramped muscles protested as she stood up and led Addie to a spot close enough to keep watch but clear of flailing hooves.

Jace didn't look at them now. All his attention was centered on Star as he cut through the last wire holding her captive.

Just like Jace had predicted, Star sensed when she was free and exploded to her feet. Eyes rolling, spinning circles like a rodeo bronco, until Jace saw an opportunity and reached for her halter.

For a moment, Sarah thought the horse was going to knock him off his feet. But apparently, Jace had ninja reflexes in addition to piloting helicopters. He planted his feet and held on until Star calmed down.

Before Sarah could stop her, Addie darted toward them. She would have thrown her arms around Star's neck if Jace hadn't stopped her.

"Easy...both of you." He blotted away the beads of moisture that dotted his brow with the back of one hand. "Sarah?"

She was already there, carefully running her hands down Star's legs and checking all four fetlocks for swelling. Other than the cuts from the wire, there didn't seem to be any injuries.

Thank You, God.

"What can I do, Mom?" There was a quaver in Addie's voice, but she lifted her chin, ready to help.

Brave girl. Braver than her mother, it seemed.

Sarah straightened. "We'll get her home and I'll call Dr. C, but I think Star is going to be just fine."

It was a slow procession back to the barn, but Sarah watched Star closely. She wasn't limping or favoring any of her limbs, which was a good sign. Jace immediately went to get a bucket of warm water while Sarah put Star in her stall, and together, they began to wash the dirt and blood from the mare's wounds.

"Stitches?" he murmured, mindful that Addie was in the tack room, searching for antibiotic ointment in the med kit.

"I don't think so, but Dr. C will know for sure."

The vet finally arrived and after a brief exam, confirmed Sarah's diagnosis.

"All Star needs is some rest from all that excitement." Dr. C looked at Sarah. "She's up to date on her tetanus shot, but keep a close eye on her over the next few days. If any of the cuts become infected, let me know and we'll get her on an antibiotic. For the rest of you?" He smiled at Addie. "I prescribe two scoops of ice cream."

Addie worked up a smile in return, but the moment Dr. C left, Sarah was stunned when Addie threw herself against Jace's broad chest and burst into tears.

"Hey, what's all this about?" Jace froze for a split second before wrapping his arms around her. "Dr. C just said that Star is going to be fine."

"It's my fault she got hurt!" Addie sobbed. "I wasn't watching her."

"You stayed with Star and kept her calm so she didn't injure herself even more. You did good, Addie Oakley."

"Daddy!" The tears subsided. Addie reared back and looked up at him reproachfully. "I told you not to call me that!"

"Did you?" He tipped his head, keenly aware that Sarah was watching the exchange, her expression unreadable.

Was it because Addie had turned to him for comfort? Or because she'd called him Daddy?

Considering what had happened, the word was a balm to the soul.

Jace had had a team of guys depending on him in difficult situations, but this one…he'd lost a decade of his life when he'd seen his daughter lying on the ground next to Star.

With every rusty wire Jace had sawed through, using a knife that wasn't *meant* to cut rusty wire, he'd prayed for a steady hand. Prayed that Addie's best friend wasn't seriously injured.

Even as he prayed, doubts had rushed in, trying to steal his concentration.

Should they wait for the vet to arrive? What if Star had broken a leg and setting her free caused more damage? Would Addie blame him? Would Sarah?

Those decisions were all on Jace and he'd felt the weight.

Then he'd asked Addie to do something difficult, too, not knowing if she would listen to him or refuse to leave Star's side.

Her trust had given Jace the courage to make that last cut.

"Addie Oakley?" Sarah finally ventured. "I don't think I've heard that one before."

"Josh Winslow calls me that." Addie grimaced. "He thinks he's being funny."

"I think he's giving you a compliment," Sarah said, trying to suppress a smile. "Annie Oakley was a brave young woman."

Addie looked doubtful, but at least she'd stopped crying.

That was good. Her tears had just about gutted Jace.

"Let's let Star rest a bit while you clean up." Sarah's gaze swept over Addie, taking in the dirt and splotches of blood on her clothing.

"That's a good idea." Jace didn't have to look in the mirror to know that he looked like a guy who'd just defused a fifteen-hundred-pound bomb with nothing but a pen knife.

"Then ice cream?" Addie was Addie again.

"Dinner first."

And Sarah was Sarah.

The world was returning to normal.

Jace glanced at his watch. Almost four hours had passed since Sarah had asked if he'd seen Addie.

"Okay." Addie peeked over the stall door to check on Star one more time before she dashed out of the barn.

"That was…" Sarah paused, searching for the right word.

Intense? Terrifying?

"Something I never want to do again," Jace said.

"Right." Sarah's teeth skimmed her lower lip. "Jace?"

Oh, oh.

He braced for impact.

They were long overdue for a conversation, but he wasn't sure he wanted to have one here. Now.

Especially if Sarah was about to tell him that he was guilty of swooping again.

But there was no way he would have let Sarah—or Addie—anywhere near Star. Risked them getting hurt.

"You...you're welcome to join us for dinner."

The mouthwatering fragrance of garlic and freshly baked bread greeted Jace as he approached the cabin.

He knocked and heard Addie's cheerful "Come in!"

Jace opened the door and stepped inside. His welcoming committee, Addie and Maisey, bounded up to him.

"Mom's making spaghetti," Addie told him.

"It smells delicious." Jace reached down to pet the border collie and spotted Sarah moving around the tiny kitchen. Her hair was loose and she'd changed into a yellow dress with narrow straps that drew attention to her sun-kissed shoulders.

This was where Jace wanted to be at the close of every day.

With Sarah and Addie.

Jace had done everything he could to prove to Sarah that he'd changed. The dinner invitation had ignited a wild hope that Sarah was beginning to trust him again. That they could become a family.

"Addie? Will you set the table, please?"

"Uh-huh."

Jace took a risk and followed Addie into the kitchen.

"You can put me to work, too."

"Oh." Sarah stumbled over the word and Jace held his breath.

Yesterday, Sarah had assigned him a task out of necessity. Working alongside each other, grilling burgers for a hungry troop of volunteers, wasn't the same as sharing her kitchen. Would she allow him in her space? Or treat him like a guest and send him back to the living room?

"I need some tomatoes cut up for the salad," she finally said. "The cutting board is in the drawer by the sink."

"Don't cut *too* many," Addie whispered. "I don't really like them."

"Neither do I," Jace whispered back.

Addie grinned.

"I heard that." Sarah opened the oven door and pulled out a sheet of breadsticks. "Tomatoes are—"

"Good for you," Addie and Jace said at the same time.

Sarah rolled her eyes, but Jace could tell she was trying not to laugh.

Jace finished the salad as Sarah filled the serving bowls and Addie arranged plates and napkins on the tablecloth. A folding chair had been placed between Sarah and Addie's.

Sarah caught Jace staring at it. "I'm sorry. That's the only one I could find—"

"It's fine." For ten years, Jace had been eating meals in the mess hall or on the sofa in his apartment and now he was here, sharing a meal with Sarah and Addie.

It was better than fine. It was a gift.

They claimed their chairs and Addie reached for Jace's hand.

"Me and Mom always hold hands when we pray."

Jace felt like an awkward middle school kid again when he glanced at Sarah. Without a word, she stretched out her hand and Jace took it, closing the circle.

Jace could get on board with this tradition.

He could get used to a lot of things.

"God, thank You for this food," Sarah murmured. "Thank You for being with Addie and Star today."

"And that Star didn't get more hurt when Dad cut the wires," Addie added under her breath.

Jace decided there was nothing more to add than a heartfelt *amen*.

Sarah's hand slipped out of his. She passed a serving bowl filled with steaming pasta and Jace's stomach rumbled in anticipation.

"Sorry." He helped himself before handing it off to Addie. "I worked through my lunch break today. My boss is kind of tough." He winked at Addie.

Sarah huffed. "Your *boss* didn't ask you to fix the roof."

Addie's eyes sparkled as she listened to the exchange.

"Tomorrow, I'm going to put out all the rocks for the scavenger hunt." She reached for the basket and helped herself to another breadstick. "You can help, Dad."

Jace glanced at Sarah.

He should have taken Sarah up on her offer to talk the night before. But Jace had been afraid the firelight, the memories, would get in the way. And that he'd end up kissing her again. He wanted to do things the right way this time.

Part of him had been delaying the inevitable, too. Waiting for a breakthrough. A sign that Sarah wanted him in her life.

He'd thought the dinner invitation might be it, but now she sat in silence.

If she wanted him to stay longer, all she had to do was say the word and Jace would call Mason. His friend would understand.

But Sarah's gaze remained trained on her plate, as if pasta was something she'd never seen before.

Jace released a slow breath.

"I'm really sorry, but I won't be able to."

"Why not?"

"I have to leave tomorrow."

Chapter Sixteen

"Leave to go where?" Addie dropped the breadstick on her plate and stared at Jace. "You said you weren't going to fly helicopters anymore!"

Sarah's head came up. Now she was looking at him almost accusingly, like he'd kept a secret from her.

What could Jace say? That he hadn't mentioned Mason's offer because he'd hoped she would ask him to stay longer?

"I'm not," Jace said carefully. "But my friend Mason offered me a job. He needs my help, too."

"But…that was before."

Before Jace had found out about her, she meant.

Oh, Addie. You're killing me here.

"What kind of job?" Sarah asked tightly.

"Mason runs an outfitter business in northern Minnesota. He takes groups out on wilderness adventures and needs a guide who can fly his plane."

At the time, it sounded like the perfect fit. Now, he couldn't imagine being anywhere else but here.

Addie's lower lip trembled. "When will you be back?"

Jace couldn't lie to her. "I'm not sure."

"There's a ton of stuff to do now that Mr. Bill can't come this summer," Addie persisted. "You can work here instead."

Jace glanced at Sarah again but this time Addie noticed.

"Right, Mom?"

"Addie...you heard what Jace said. He has a job. His friend needs him—"

"So do we!" Addie's chair tipped sideways as she pushed to her feet. "You don't want him to stay! I can tell! You never told Dad about me or he would have come back a long time ago. He said so!"

"Addie, please sit down." Sarah's voice shook.

"I'm not hungry anymore." Addie bounded toward her bedroom and the door slammed shut behind her.

Jace started to follow, but Sarah stepped in his path.

He wanted to protest, but the pain in Sarah's eyes sliced through him.

Pain he'd caused.

Even if he hadn't witnessed the deep bond between mother and daughter, Sarah's stricken expression told Jace that Addie's outburst was rare.

"I should talk to her."

"Addie's upset, Jace." Sarah crossed her arms in front of her chest as if she was trying to hold herself together. "She needs some time alone. I'd told her that you were only staying for two weeks but...but I had no idea she thought that had changed."

Well, Jace had been hoping—praying—it would, too.

But Sarah's silence at the table had spoken volumes.

For Addie's sake, Sarah would let Jace be involved in her life, but she still didn't trust him. Maybe she never would.

Jace had promised her that he wouldn't do anything to hurt Addie, but the muffled sobs coming from the bedroom told Jace he'd broken that one, too.

And now Jace had caused a rift between mother and daughter, something he'd never intended.

Maybe it *was* time to leave.

Sarah saw Jace glance at Addie's door.

She'd told him that Addie needed time to process things, but so did Sarah.

After the events of the day, she'd forgotten that tomorrow was officially Jace's last day. Addie might not be ready to talk, but she and Jace had to.

Except… Jace was walking toward the door. Right before he reached it, he looked back at Sarah.

"I have to get an early start tomorrow, but I'd like to say goodbye first, if that's all right."

Hurt bloomed in Sarah's chest.

The take-charge pilot didn't want to discuss how they could make this work for their daughter? Wasn't going to make plans to see Addie again?

Sarah forced a nod. "The college students will be here at nine for registration orientation."

"I plan on being on the road before that." Jace's gaze drifted to Addie's door again. "I'm sorry, Sarah. I never…" He paused and blew out a sigh. "I'm sorry."

The last time Jace had left Four Arrows, he hadn't apologized, but it didn't make the ache in Sarah's chest go away.

The door closed behind him and Sarah collapsed on the sofa.

Why hadn't Jace told her that he was no longer in the army? *Because what he does or doesn't do isn't any of your business*, she chided herself. *You knew he was leaving.*

But she hadn't expected it to hurt so much.

After witnessing Addie's meltdown, had Jace decided that parenting was more difficult than he thought it would be?

Even as the thought flitted through Sarah's mind, she felt a stab of guilt.

There was no doubt in her mind that Jace loved Addie.

Addie's door opened a crack. "Mom?"

Sarah blinked away her tears and held out her arms.

It was all Addie needed to see. She crossed the distance that separated them in a single bound, landed on the sofa and burrowed against Sarah's side.

"I'm sorry for what I said." Her red-rimmed eyes filled with tears. "I didn't mean it."

"I know." Sarah slipped her arms around Addie and held on tight. "We're all guilty of that sometimes, sweetheart."

And sometimes, a person remained silent when she should have spoken up.

But what good would it have done?

Other than the kiss, Jace had never told Sarah that he cared about her. Never said that his promise to Maggie wasn't the only thing that had kept him at Four Arrows.

Sarah had been devastated the first time he'd left. What if she'd told him that she had feelings for him, only to have him reject her again?

"I don't want Dad to leave," Addie whispered.

"I know you don't." Sarah brushed a damp strand of copper hair from Addie's cheek. "But Jace...your dad...he has a life. A job. He doesn't live at Four Arrows."

"He could if you got married."

Sarah's breath stalled in her lungs. Is that why Addie had reacted so strongly? She'd imagined them becoming a real family? "A couple has to be in love before they get married."

"You loved each other once."

The words scraped across a wound Sarah thought had healed.

She'd told Jace she loved him, but it wasn't until after he'd left that she realized he'd kissed her instead of saying it back.

"Your dad loves *you*," Sarah said softly. "That's what matters."

Addie sniffled. "He didn't say when he was coming back."

Sarah had no answer for that. She couldn't imagine Jace turning his back on Addie, though.

"I have an idea. There's still plenty of daylight left. Why don't we saddle the horses and find places for your painted rocks now?"

"I can't ride Star, though."

"Not until next week, no, but Pancakes would love to get out and stretch his legs."

Addie snuggled against Sarah. "Thor?"

"Next year."

"Okay." Another tear leaked from the corner of Addie's eye and she brushed it away.

"Why don't you find a container for the rocks and I'll clean up from dinner?" Sarah pressed another kiss against Addie's temple, thankful for a respite, however brief, from the storm.

Addie disappeared into her room and Sarah walked over to the table.

You could get married.

When Jace had taken Sarah's hand before they'd prayed, she'd let herself imagine what it would be like to sit down together at the table every day. Watch sunsets and sunrises. Share the rollercoaster ride of parenting a sweet but precocious ten-year-old.

But once again, Jace's plans didn't include a family. He might have changed careers, but that didn't mean Jace had changed. Wilderness adventures was the perfect fit for a man who loved to fly. If Jace needed a daily rush of adrenaline, the most Sarah could offer was a three-mile hike to Maple Hill.

She rinsed the dishes and set them in the sink to deal with after Addie went to bed.

They walked to the barn together and Sarah held her breath when Addie's gaze strayed to the lodge.

Would she ask if Jace could join them?

Sarah wasn't sure she could face him right now. Not until she'd had time to detangle all the thoughts in her head.

Addie didn't say anything and Sarah wondered if her daughter needed some time to think, too.

Fortunately, an evening trail ride was a good place for that.

Sarah whistled for Autumn and the mare trotted over to the fence. She saddled the mare and chose a gentle eight-year-old named Teddy for Addie instead of Pancakes, who was more interested in a quiet dinner served in his stall.

Sarah tucked the container of rocks in her saddlebag before she mounted. As they started out, the sun sank lower, painting the sky with a backdrop of apricot, rose and lavender.

She always smiled when campers commented on the peace and quiet of the forest. Sarah didn't think it was quiet at all. Birds sang in the trees and the spring peepers performed a boisterous chorus in the reeds at the edge of the lake. As for peace… Sarah was trying.

"It was so scary…what happened to Star."

Sarah twisted in the saddle to look at Addie. She hadn't considered that taking the same trail would conjure up the images of the long walk back to the barn after their ordeal.

"We can go another way."

Addie shook her head. "I want to remember this instead." She pulled back on the reins and slipped off the saddle to retrieve the first rock from the saddlebag.

Sarah's eyes stung even as pride welled up inside her. Jace had told Sarah she was raising an amazing child, but Sarah saw a lot of Jace in Addie, too.

He hadn't let the past harden his heart. No one—not even Sarah—had expected the seeds of faith sown that summer at Four Arrows would find soft ground, but they had.

No wonder she'd fallen in love with him all over again.

"Mom?" Addie sounded worried. "You have a funny look on your face. Are you okay?"

Not even close.

Sarah nodded anyway. "The mosquitos are coming out, so we should keep going."

An hour later, Addie had scattered rocks all the way to Maple Hill. By the time the round pen came into view, shadows crossed the trail and collected in the pockets between the trees.

Autumn shied off the path as Sarah suddenly jerked back on

the reins. She patted the mare's neck in apology and the mare relaxed, but Sarah's heart continued to beat in double time.

Jace's truck was parked by the barn. He stood by the door, waiting for them.

Addie slid down from the saddle but she didn't run over to greet him. Her expression turned wary.

Maybe because she'd also figured out why Jace was there.

He'd decided not to wait until morning to leave.

The shadows concealed Sarah's expression, but Jace saw the tension in her shoulders as she dismounted.

"I'll check on Star."

She knew. And she was giving him an opportunity to talk to Addie alone, but Jace had to remind himself to breathe.

Tears glistened in Addie's eyes. "You're leaving now, aren't you?"

And Jace thought saying goodbye ten years ago was hard.

It seemed he had a knack for making the Crosse girls cry.

When Jace had returned to the lodge, he'd decided there was no point in prolonging the inevitable. He wasn't going to get a wink of sleep anyway, so he may as well put some miles on the truck.

"I left my phone number and my new address in Maggie's office. You can call or text me anytime."

"It isn't the same," Addie said in a small voice.

"Come here." Jace pulled his daughter into a hug. When Addie finally let go, Jace lost another chunk of his heart.

"Love you, Addison Margaret Ellen Crosse."

"I love you, too." Addie gifted him with a watery smile.

"Let's go find your mom."

Sarah emerged from Star's stall before they reached it.

Tiny lines fanned out from the corners of her eyes and the frown that had settled between her brows when she'd seen him standing by the barn hadn't gone away.

Because you're still here, Jace reminded himself.

"Dad has to leave tonight," Addie told her.

Jace sucked in a quiet breath when Sarah held out her hand.

"Thank you for all your help the past two weeks."

Jace shook it. *Shook* it. When all he wanted to do was pull her into his arms.

"You're welcome."

They'd turned into polite strangers now instead of…whatever they'd been the past two weeks. Coworkers? Friends?

Jace had wanted more.

He still wanted more.

There was a lot to pray about. How to be in Addie's life when Sarah didn't want him to be part of hers. What it would look like. Because Jace already knew what it felt like.

Trust in the Lord with all your heart… He will make your paths straight.

Jace bent down and gave Addie one more hug.

They escorted Jace to the truck, Sarah keeping a few feet of distance between them while Addie clung to his hand.

He paused before he got into the truck, but Sarah didn't say anything. Not when he closed the door. Started the engine.

Drove away.

Jace knew if he glanced in the rearview mirror, he'd pull a U-turn in the middle of the road.

He had to trust that God was still guiding his path…even if that path took him away from Four Arrows.

Chapter Seventeen

You can do this, Sarah.

Key in hand, she walked up the steps to the lodge.

The steps Jace had fixed.

Yesterday, at orientation for the new staffers, she'd had to deal with a flurry of last-minute details. Stocking the General Store with new merchandise. Setting up the registration table. A tour of the property for the college students who weren't familiar with the layout of the camp.

In the chaos, Sarah hadn't had time to think about Jace. Much.

So far, Sarah had avoided the infirmary and the upstairs apartment, but it didn't matter. She'd thought Jace's absence would staunch the flow of memories, not realizing there would be new ones. No matter where Sarah went, Jace was there. The barn. The archery range. The patio. Her kitchen.

Maggie's office.

After he'd left, Sarah had found a note with Jace's phone number and address on the desk—along with one of Addie's painted rocks.

TRUST.

She didn't know where or when he'd found it, but Addie insisted on keeping it, so the bright yellow missive was the first thing Sarah saw when she stepped into the room.

Thankfully, in a few hours, Sarah would be caught in the whirlwind of opening day. She'd set her alarm an hour earlier than usual so she could concentrate on the campers when they arrived.

She turned her attention to the stack of cardboard boxes filled with T-shirts that her registration team would be handing out to campers when they arrived. The shipment, which had sat in a distribution center for several weeks, had arrived during the middle of Sarah's training session. She hadn't had time to sort through colors and sizes until now.

While she was searching for something to cut though the packaging tape on the box, her cell phone began to ring. Sarah's heart jumped when she saw the name flashing on the screen. She hadn't talked to her father in months. The last time she had, he was working at a clinic in the Philippines.

"Hi, Dad."

There was a split second of silence. "Sarah. I wasn't sure you'd be awake this early."

"The first campers arrive today." Not that her father paid attention to things like that—or holidays or birthdays, for that matter—but there'd been a tiny flicker of hope that he'd remembered and was calling to find out if she was ready for the summer season.

"I won't keep you long. There will be a line outside the clinic before it opens."

"It sounds like it's going well."

"We treated over a hundred patients yesterday." A hint of pride crept into his voice. "The director asked if I'd be interested in opening another clinic a few hours away. It means more hours, but there's such a need for quality medical care, I can't say no."

"That's great, Dad." Sarah meant it, even though it was still hard to accept the fact that Franklin Crosse's compassion extended to everyone but his family.

"I spoke with Melanie yesterday."

Melanie Raeburn had been the receptionist at the clinic in Crosse Creek. She wasn't happy when Sarah's father had announced he was closing his private practice to work for an organization that paired doctors with communities in need. And since the announcement had come only a few months after Sarah had found out she was pregnant, Sarah had always felt Melanie blamed her for the decision.

"I haven't seen her in a while. How is she?"

"Concerned about you."

"Me?" Sarah frowned. "Why?"

"She heard that Jace Marshall was in town."

So, of course, the head gardener of Crosse Creek's grapevine had to find out if it was true.

Sarah's grip on her cell tightened. Her father had been livid when he'd found out that Jace was Addie's father, but as far as she knew, he hadn't told anyone else.

"Sarah? Please tell me that isn't true."

"He came back to see Maggie."

"I'm sure that's what he claimed. How convenient that she was gone and you're in charge of the camp now. I'm sure Marshall found out how much the property is worth before he showed up at the door."

"Jace isn't like that."

"You know exactly what he's like," her father retorted. "He left you, Sarah."

"So did you."

Sarah wasn't sure he'd heard her, or if it didn't matter, because he kept on going.

"I don't know what you ever saw in him, but I thought I'd gotten through to Marshall." Her father's voice picked up steam. "Did you tell him about Addie? If you did, you'll never get rid of him. The guy is probably looking for someone to pay the bills."

The irony wasn't lost on Sarah. She barely had enough money to cover her own.

Sarah pressed her hand against her forehead. "Jace joined the military, Dad. He's a decorated pilot, not someone looking for a handout…and what does that mean? You thought you'd gotten through to Jace?"

"I'd asked Maggie to keep an eye on you because I was afraid you would throw your future away on that boy," her father said. "Maggie told me to trust you, but I didn't trust Marshall, so I sought him out and we had a conversation."

Sarah's mouth went dry. "What did you tell him?"

Jace had never mentioned they'd even met, but knowing her father, it had been a lecture, not a conversation.

"The truth. That you'd wanted to be a doctor since you were eight years old and he would only get in the way of your goals if he stuck around. He knew you were better off without him."

Because Dr. Crosse, a respected physician in town, had said it was so?

Sarah's hands were shaking so hard she almost lost her grip on the phone. "Dad…why would you do that to Jace?"

"I didn't do anything to Jace," he sputtered. "I intervened on behalf of my daughter. Not that it did any good."

Sarah decided to ignore the barb.

"When did you talk to him? Jace never came to the house."

"I stopped by the camp. We had a conversation and Jace told me he was leaving that day anyway, so I didn't have to worry."

They'd had a conversation. And then Jace had texted Sarah, asking her to meet him by the old homestead.

"I have to open the clinic now." Her father's voice sounded brisk, professional. As if he'd just crossed off an item on his to-do list. "I care about you, Sarah," he added stiffly. "Don't make another mistake and let Jace Marshall back into your life."

Sarah thought of all the times Jace had made her laugh. The

way he'd worked with quiet efficiency without accepting anything in return. How he'd swooped in and become Addie's hero.

She hung up the phone and closed her eyes.

Maybe the mistake hadn't been letting Jace back into her life. Maybe the mistake was letting him go.

Was it possible Jace had been lying when he'd told Sarah that he didn't care about her?

He'd referred to himself as "trouble" more than once, but Sarah got the impression Jace had decided if he couldn't shake the label, he would wear it with pride. Sarah had seen through the act, though. Jace didn't want to be defined by his case file.

And yet, he'd left again, without making any promises. Not even to Addie.

"Good morning!"

Bryce and his wife, Aimee, stood in the doorway. Aimee held out a travel mug.

"We thought you might need some caffeine and a few extra hands this morning."

"I—" Sarah was about to say "have everything under control," but the boxes on the floor said otherwise. "Could definitely use both."

Bryce grinned. "I think some more volunteers will show up today, but we're early risers, so put us to work."

Sarah let Aimee press the cup of coffee in her hands.

"Thank you." The warmth spread through Sarah, overtaking the chill that had settled in her bones during the conversation with her father.

"I have to set up the refreshment table in the cafeteria before Addie wakes up," Sarah said. "If you could unpack these T-shirts and sort them by size, that would be great."

"We're on it!"

Sarah left the couple alone and paused in front of the registration table. Addie had painted a colorful welcome banner for opening day and decorated the counselors' lanyards with stickers. In a few hours, the camp would be flooded with third and fourth graders, their counselors and support staff.

Maggie would have been in the thick of it all, her warm smile putting even the most nervous campers at ease while Sarah had been content to stay in the background. Content? Or hiding?

She wasn't sure anymore.

Sarah veered onto the path that led to the cafeteria.

The first group of campers was bringing their own kitchen staff, so all Sarah had to do was make sure the pantry was stocked with the menu items she'd been given and check in on them to make sure things were going well.

This week.

God's got this, Maggie liked to say. A reminder that He was in control. Sarah believed that, but she hadn't embraced the rest of it. *Because He's got us. We're safe. Held in the palm of His hand.*

So why had she been living as if she'd somehow slipped through His fingers and had to do everything alone?

Hope. Breathe. Take Courage. Pray Big.

Sarah wanted to collect them in her heart like the rocks Addie had hidden along the trail.

Okay, God. Two hours until the gate opens. I don't know what this summer is going to look like, but I know You're here and I'm going to trust You.

"Mom?" Addie landed beside Sarah. "Can I stay a little longer? The counselors are going to have a karaoke contest!"

Sarah wasn't about to say no. They'd had a long talk after Jace had left and while Addie seemed to understand that it was important he kept his commitment to his friend, just like he'd kept his promise to Maggie, the sparkle in her daughter's eyes had dimmed.

"Go ahead. I'll check on Star."

"Thanks." Addie returned to the firepit, where she was immediately surrounded by a pack of first-time campers who'd already adopted Addie as their "big sister" for the week.

Pastor Bryce and Aimee had stayed through dinner, along with Lindy and her father, who'd been commandeered by Lindy into giving fishing lessons after the meal.

The laughter and music faded as Sarah made her way to the barn. Star was doing remarkably well, but Sarah was still concerned about infection.

She reached the door, only to find it blocked by an enormous cardboard box.

Sarah hadn't seen a delivery truck, but she'd spent most of the evening down at the waterfront, watching the canoe races.

She tried to lift it—too heavy—and ended up pushing the box through the open door and into the barn. There was no name on it, but the feed store's logo was stamped in the upper corner.

Sarah's lips curved in a smile.

She'd planned on picking up her order, but Val, who lived a few miles down the road from the camp, must have taken a short detour on her way home.

Pancakes stretched his neck over the stall and nickered, reminding Sarah that dinner was ten minutes late.

"Just a minute, buddy." She sliced through the packing tape and peeled back the flaps. Sucked in a breath.

Nestled inside was a brand-new trail saddle, a constellation of tiny silver stars hand-tooled in the gleaming leather.

Val didn't make mistakes, so there was only one person who could have sent it.

Hands shaking, Sarah pulled out the card.

Happy Birthdays.

Sarah refused to cry. Except…it was too late. A tear cut a jagged path down her cheek.

"No," she said out loud, even though Jace was two hundred miles away. "You can't do nice things and…and not be here."

She closed the flaps on the box, grabbed the med kit from the tack room and strode toward Star's stall.

The mare, who wasn't used to being confined, thumped her hoof against the floor, the equine equivalent of filing a formal complaint.

"I know you're frustrated, baby." Sarah was frustrated, too. Because Jace was frustrating. Confusing. Thoughtful...

And she was crying again.

"Sarah?" Lindy's lilting voice echoed through the barn.

"In here." Sarah swiped at another rogue tear before Lindy reached the stall.

"Addie said you were here, and I wanted to say goodbye before I left." Fortunately, Lindy's attention shifted to Star, who'd shuffled closer to greet her newest visitor. "This must be Star." She gently rubbed the mare's nose. "Addie told me about her, too. Is she doing all right?"

"Better," Sarah said.

"It must have been a pretty scary situation, with Jace having to cut through the barbed wire to free her."

An image of Jace kneeling on the ground, his face inches from Star's hooves as he painstakingly cut through each wire, flashed in Sarah's mind. And then he'd asked Addie to trust him.

Another tear leaked out. This one Lindy noticed.

"Sarah." She grimaced. "I'm so sorry. I didn't mean to stir up a bad memory."

"You didn't." Sarah tried on a smile and felt it slip sideways. "Star will be fine."

"What about you?"

Sarah wanted to laugh, but something in Lindy's compassionate gaze required honesty.

"I'm not sure yet."

"Jace left, didn't he?"

All Sarah had to do was nod. Answer the question with a simple yes. But words began to pour out instead.

She told Lindy about the summer she'd fallen in love with Jace, and what Jace had said to her the day he'd left. The phone call from her father that morning.

"I don't know why Jace never told me about their conversation," Sarah finally said. "I would have stood up for him."

"It sounds to me like Jace had a rough childhood," Lindy said carefully. "Not that it's an excuse, but if he believed he wasn't good enough for you, it would explain why he left. He was protecting you from himself."

"The first time," Sarah whispered. "But he did it again. If Jace cared about me, wouldn't he have stayed?"

"Did you ask him to?"

Sarah blinked. "N-no."

Because she'd been afraid Jace would reject her again.

And maybe…he'd been afraid of the same thing.

"Do you think…"

A smile backlit Lindy's eyes.

"There's only one way to find out."

Jace stuffed another hoodie in his duffel bag and zipped it shut.

The upside of not owning many possessions. It didn't take long to pack.

"Knock knock."

Jace rolled his eyes at Mason.

"You know, it's not *really* knocking when all you do is say the words while you're strolling into the room," he told his friend.

"I don't stroll." Mason grinned. "I walk with authority."

Jace couldn't argue with that.

Mason towered above Jace by at least three inches, with a linebacker's build. If his size wasn't intimidating enough, a jagged scar cut a path from his left cheekbone to his chin, a trophy from the college hockey he'd played before enlisting.

"What's up?" Jace wasn't in the mood for chitchat. He'd just returned from what Mason had billed as the Canoe and Camping Excursion. In reality, it had involved keeping a group of city guys, who'd decided a few days in the wilderness would make for an epic bachelor party, alive.

Jace had successfully completed the op, but not without wrapping one sprained ankle, dealing with an outbreak of poison sumac and treating several cases of sheer stupidity.

"You skipped lunch," Mason said.

"Are you the calorie police?"

"It's the most important meal of the day."

"I thought that was breakfast."

"Every meal is important." Mason patted his washboard abs. "But I came by to deliver this." He reached into the pocket of his nylon hiking pants and handed Jace an envelope.

"If this is a bonus for keeping those idiot groomsmen from lighting themselves on fire, I'm telling you right now it's not enough."

Mason crossed his arms and speared Jace with the narrow-eyed glare that had brought more than one raw recruit to tears.

"Such a funny guy. Just open it, Falcon."

"Yes, sir." Jace saluted in response to his call sign. Ran his thumb through the seal and pulled out...a postcard. Two words jumped out at him.

One wish.

His mouth dried up like he'd just swallowed a bucket of sand.

The night he'd arrived in Minnesota, Mason had lit a campfire and used all his skills of interrogation to get Jace to open up about his time at Four Arrows.

He knew about Addie's postcard. Sarah's struggles keeping the camp solvent financially. The guilt he'd felt when Addie had accused Sarah of not wanting him to stay. Everything. Jace might have even mentioned the plot of *Anne of Green Gables*, for crying out loud.

"What's this?" If it was Mason's way of getting him to lighten up, Jace couldn't work up a smile, let alone a laugh.

Mason leaned forward and pretended to study it. "A postcard?"

"Are you messing with me?"

Mason put up his hands. "Have I ever... Never mind. I'm not messing with you."

Maybe. But the smirk on his friend's face told Jace something was up.

He flipped the card over but there was nothing else written on it. No stamp or return address on the envelope, either.

"How...*where* did it come from?"

Mason was grinning again. "Special delivery. Move it, Falcon." He pointed to the door.

But Jace couldn't move.

Because Sarah and Addie stood in the doorway.

Chapter Eighteen

Sarah. And. Addie.

Jace's mouth opened and closed again.

Addie broke the silence with a cheerful "Surprise!"

Now Jace moved. He opened his arms and Addie flew toward him. Jace caught her up in a hug that lifted her off her feet.

Jace's only link to the outside world over the past week was a satellite phone, but if there'd been some kind of emergency at Four Arrows, Mason would have contacted him.

His gaze shifted to Addie. The tip of her nose was sunburned, but other than that, she looked fine.

And Sarah...

She was wearing a loose-fitting dress and a pair of cowboy boots. Red cowboy boots, identical to the ones she'd worn for the talent show years ago. The one Jace had skipped because he'd been so jealous of Ian, who'd stepped up and volunteered to share the stage with Sarah.

Jace had seen mirages before. Rivers of shimmering water that cut a path through the sand dunes before they disappeared. Sarah—her smile beautiful but a little uncertain—was real.

But why was she *here*?

Mason cleared his throat and Jace realized he was staring.

He tore his gaze away from Sarah and smacked into his friend's knowing grin.

"Addie?" Mason boomed. "How would you like to meet my sled dogs?"

Addie's face lit up. "Yes!"

"If your mom and dad don't mind, that is…" Mason waited and when neither one of them said anything, he continued, "Great. I'll show Addie the ropes course afterward. She's not afraid of heights, is she?" He winked at Addie and she giggled. "No? It's all good? Okay. Let's go, Carrots."

Addie followed Mason outside and the screen door snapped shut behind them.

"You're here." Jace was glad Mason hadn't stuck around or his new call sign would be Captain Obvious.

Instead of responding—or laughing—Sarah scanned the interior of the cabin.

"This is nice. I like the stone fireplace."

Jace hadn't paid much attention to his surroundings. One of the perks of his new job was having a cabin to himself, but he'd rather babysit a bunch of *Survivor* wannabes than feel the walls close in on him while his memory replayed every moment he'd been at Four Arrows.

"Mason's grandparents built the cabins. He took over when they retired and did some updates, but the guests like the rustic feel." Jace doubted Sarah had driven seven hours to talk about Mason's decor, though. "Is everything all right at the camp? How is it you were able to leave?"

Why are you here was the question Jace really wanted to ask.

"The first group left yesterday, and the next one won't be arriving until tomorrow. Bryce and his wife offered to camp-sit until I get back. They're taking care of the horses and Maisey."

"Star?"

"Getting spoiled from all the extra attention, but there's no sign of infection."

"And opening day? How did that go?"

Sarah's teeth skimmed over her lower lip.

Oh, oh.

"The new counselors are great, and thanks to Bryce, I had more than enough volunteers," she finally said.

"But—"

"My dad called."

Wow. Jace raked his hand through his hair. "I'm guessing it wasn't to cheer you on for another season."

"No. He...he actually called because of you."

"Me."

"Melanie, his former receptionist, took it upon herself to let him know that you were in Crosse Creek."

Based on Sarah's expression, the conversation hadn't gone well.

Jace had been concerned about rumors starting, but he didn't think the local grapevine would stretch across the ocean.

"I'm sorry." But then again, Jace's MO seemed to be causing trouble for Sarah.

"I'm not." Sarah caught his gaze, held it. "You never said anything about having a conversation with him."

Technically, it hadn't been a conversation. Dr. Crosse had talked while Jace listened.

"He had a right to be concerned."

Sarah's dad was the only parent she had. Jace could tell that Sarah yearned for his approval and support. The doctor was a perfectionist, but he wanted the best for Sarah and they'd both known it wasn't Jace.

"What did he say?"

"It doesn't matter now."

But the expression on Sarah's face told Jace that it did.

"Nothing that I didn't already know, all right? I wasn't in a good place when we met. I would have dragged you down."

Sarah's hands rolled into fists at her side. "When did he talk to you?"

"Sarah—"

"The day you left?"

Jace nodded.

"The day you pointed out that you'd never made any promises?" she pressed. "When you said what we'd had was…was fun?"

The memory of the last time he'd seen Sarah was buried deep, but the pain in her eyes pushed it to the surface.

Jace had texted Sarah, asking her to meet him at the old homestead when she came back from the morning trail ride. Jace had gotten there first, angry and frustrated because Dr. Crosse had tracked him down and coolly listed all the reasons why Jace would ruin Sarah's life if he stayed in Crosse Creek.

The old Jace might have stayed out of sheer defiance, to teach the old man a lesson about interfering in his business. Then Jace had remembered holding Sarah in his arms the night before. Hearing her whispered *I love you*.

The only reason Sarah would let him go was if she thought it was what *he* wanted.

Jace had seen her ambling down the trail, cheeks flushed with color, a smile on her face. Happy.

The weight of making sure she stayed that way had pressed down hard.

Sarah has dreamed of being a doctor since she was a child. What are your plans for the future?

Jace had had the seed of a dream only, planted during the countless hours he'd spent in front of the television as a kid, watching movies about heroes who fought for freedom and country.

For Sarah, Jace had dared to share that plan with her father. Instead of looking impressed, he'd said, "What makes you think they'll want you?"

And then he'd laughed.

Just like Jace had laughed, when Sarah had refused to accept that their relationship was over.

It had just about killed him, but it had worked. She'd stumbled away from Jace as if he'd physically struck her.

The only thing that had kept Jace from chasing Sarah back to the camp was knowing she'd have a better life without him.

But he couldn't let Sarah go on thinking she hadn't mattered to him.

"Yes." Jace answered her questions. "But I lied."

"You…lied?" Sarah stared at Jace.

After talking to Lindy, she suspected he had. But hearing him admit it… She swallowed hard.

"Why?"

"Why?" Jace repeated. "Because I could barely take care of myself, let alone anyone else, and your dad knew it."

No, Jace hadn't fit into her father's plans for Sarah's life.

"You should have told me that he came to see you."

"For once… I had to do the right thing. Your dad said you'd stopped studying for your online classes. That you didn't seem excited about college." Jace paused. "I was the rebel, but I knew how strong you were. I knew you'd defend me, no matter what your dad thought."

"You were worth defending."

"And you were better off without me," Jace said quietly.

"Don't you think I should have had a say in that? You didn't have to protect me from myself, Jace."

"Until I met you, I pretty much messed up everything. I wasn't protecting you from yourself. I was protecting you from *me*."

Understanding dawned.

"You did it again, didn't you?" Sarah whispered. "You decided we were better off without you. That's why you didn't make plans to see Addie again."

"I told you about my dad. I didn't have the best parenting role model when I was growing up," Jace said tightly. "The last thing I want to do is cause a rift between the two of you, like I did with you and your dad."

"You didn't cause the rift," Sarah said. "My dad is doing what he loves but he has a hard time accepting that I am, too. When I met you, I was already having second thoughts about being a doctor." What she'd never had was second thoughts about loving Jace.

Sarah released a low laugh. "We aren't opposites, Jace. The truth is, we're a lot alike. We've never felt like we're good enough. But God has put some people in my path recently who reminded me that God settled the question of my worth a long time ago. I'm not alone. I'm loved...redeemed by His grace. It's time I started living that way.

"After Maggie died, I didn't reach out to people for help because I wanted to prove that she hadn't made a mistake when she'd entrusted Four Arrows to me. But it was more than that. I was afraid of being rejected. You talk about all the mistakes you've made, but I've made some, too." *Courage, Sarah.* "I should have told you about Addie ten years ago...and last week, I should have asked you to stay."

The slow smile that spread across Jace's face sent the butterflies in Sarah's stomach into motion.

"I know that you have a new job," she added quickly. Sarah had noticed the duffel bag on his bunk and it looked as if he was packing for another trip. "But we can set up a visitation schedule so you can see Addie..."

Jace was shaking his head. "I don't think so."

Jace saw Sarah's expression fall and hurried to explain himself.

"Number one, I don't have a job. Mason said he doesn't trust me to fly his plane because I'm so twitterpated—his word, not mine—that I can't see straight. He fired me when I got back last night."

"Fired you?"

"Uh-huh. What he didn't know was that I'd already decided to quit." Jace crossed the distance between them. "I thought I could…come back. Get better at being a dad. Cut some firewood. Take care of the grounds."

"You are an amazing dad," Sarah said. Her lips curved in the mischievous smile he remembered. "But I do need a caretaker."

"Good, because I need you." Jace couldn't believe how good it felt to say the words. "I love you, Sarah. I always have."

Sarah's eyes misted. "I love you, too."

Her gaze dropped to the card Jace was still holding in his hand.

"That was my wish, you know. You coming home."

Home.

Jace let the word sink deep.

"I have more than one," he murmured, drawing her into the circle of his arms. "Campfires. Trail rides. Beating you at archery. Teaching Addie how to drive a car. Scaring boys like Josh Winslow away." Jace tucked a strand of loose hair behind Sarah's ear and felt her shiver. "Gazillions of kisses."

Sarah reached up, framed his face in her hands.

"I can make that one come true right away."

And she did.

When the kiss ended, they were both breathless.

"Will Addie be happy?" Jace murmured against her hair.

"She loves you." Sarah tried to look stern. "And not because you bought her a new saddle. Or sent a donation that will keep the horses in feed for another year."

"That donation was anonymous."

"Mmm." She peeked up at him through her lashes. "Then how did you know about it?"

She had him there.

"Taking care of you and Addie is my new mission."

"There's taking care of…and then there's spoiling." Sarah tried to look severe and failed.

"I have ten years to make up for."

"Fine." Sarah gave in. "A little spoiling."

Jace was looking forward to it. He was looking forward to a lot of things.

"Jace… I've been praying a lot, and I think God wants me to keep Four Arrows going. Not because Maggie entrusted it to me, but because her legacy isn't just a piece of property. It's about the people. I want to be part of that, even if it isn't always easy."

Jace had been praying about the future of the camp, too. Maggie's legacy wasn't just the camp, it was her willingness to trust God. To share the blessings she'd been given.

"I want to be part of that, too," he told Sarah.

Laughter danced in her eyes. "I can't pay you very much."

"Doesn't matter. I get to be with you, so the benefits outweigh the risks." Jace reached for her hand. "Should we tell Addie?"

"That you're coming back to Four Arrows?"

Jace kissed her again.

"That we're going home…together."

Chapter Nineteen

"Hurry up, Mom!"

Sarah, who'd been reading through the roster of the campers scheduled to arrive for the first equine camp, looked up as Addie appeared in the doorway.

"Five more minutes."

"You said that five minutes ago!"

"What's the rush?"

"Dad said he'd go with us, but he thinks we should go now, because it might rain."

Sarah supposed she could cut it down to three. Or two. And not because she was afraid of a summer shower.

She hadn't seen Jace for several hours—not that she'd been counting—but suddenly, a walk in the woods with her two favorite people sounded like the perfect addition to her to-do list.

"I'll meet you by the barn in…a minute."

"Okay!" Addie grinned and disappeared again.

Sarah finished separating the campers into groups based on their riding experience and shut down the file.

A new background appeared on the computer screen and she shook her head, even as a smile emerged. Sarah never caught Jace in the act, but every time she sat down at the desk, a new photo appeared. This one, a selfie of the three of them fishing from the canoe that Addie had taken with Jace's cell phone.

The three of them, making new memories.

Sarah still had a hard time believing it.

Thank You, Lord.

"Hi, Sarah!" Taylor, one of the college-age counselors, waved to her from the General Store. She'd volunteered to restock the shelves with the herd of stuffed horses Sarah had added to the inventory. The last group of campers had bought every single one, so this time, Sarah had doubled the order.

She'd borrowed the brilliant idea from Mason, who sold plush replicas of his sled dogs to the guests who stayed at the lodge. All the money went directly into a fund to offset the cost of the teams' care. Knowing that both children and adults loved souvenirs of their stay at camp, Sarah had decided to give it a try. Every little bit helped, especially now that she'd told Tom Jensen she wouldn't be selling any of the horses.

That decision had been a step of faith, too, but one Sarah felt at peace with. Jace had pointed out that instead of reducing the team, she should think about adding more equine camps that extended past the busy summer season.

For the first time since Maggie's death, the future didn't seem as uncertain. The challenges, not quite so challenging.

Because Sarah wasn't facing them alone.

She stepped outside and her heart performed a familiar somersault in her chest when she spotted Jace walking out of the barn.

No longer the outsider he'd once claimed to be, he fit right in at Four Arrows, from his T-shirt with the camp logo all the way down to the hiking boots on his feet.

Sarah had offered Jace the use of a cabin, but instead he'd moved into Maggie's upstairs apartment, where he could keep a watchful eye on things. In the week since he'd returned, Jace had also tamed the grounds, taught archery lessons and put out at least a dozen little fires every day, with Addie attached to him like a shadow.

Sarah wouldn't want it any other way.

She started across the lawn and the movement drew Jace's attention. The slow smile she'd fallen in love with tipped the corners of his lips.

Jace, always mindful of her reputation, leaned forward and planted a chaste kiss on Sarah's forehead.

"Where's Addie?" Sarah looked around, but there was no sign of their daughter.

"She ran back to the cabin. She decided this would be a good time to hide the rocks she painted yesterday. Since it's an equine camp, she was hoping we could leave some near the chapel this time. That way, the campers will find them when you stop there for prayer and praise time."

"Jace Marshall," she teased. "You looked at my activity calendar."

"Looked at it? I memorized it. How else will I know when I can steal you away?" The warmth in his eyes spiked the outside temperature a few degrees higher.

Sarah had discovered that Jace loved to make her blush as often as he made her laugh.

She tipped her head back. The bank of gray clouds that blocked the sunlight had begun to disperse, revealing patches of blue sky.

"It doesn't look like rain anymore, and it would be good for the horses to stretch their legs before camp starts tomorrow."

"Uh-huh. I was thinking we could walk this time." Jace's voice dropped. "It would take longer, and I've missed you."

"I've missed you, too," Sarah murmured. The past few days, their various responsibilities had kept them on opposite sides of the camp. "Walking it is."

Addie dashed up to them, a backpack slung over her shoulder.

She was already six steps ahead of Jace and Sarah before she looked over her shoulder. "Let's go!"

Sarah shot Jace a sideways glance. "Can you keep up, Falcon?"

Thanks to Mason, she knew his call sign. And it fit him a lot better than Mr. Serious.

Jace released a low laugh. "Not even if I had my chopper."

Addie forged ahead of them and Jace reached for Sarah's hand.

"Ready for tomorrow?"

"Getting there." Sarah sighed. "It helped that Bryce found someone to take over the kitchen this week. I don't know what will happen after that, but—"

"God does."

"Right." Sarah smiled. "One step at a time."

They rounded a bend in the path and saw Addie hiding a rock in a patch of daylilies growing next to the chapel.

"Addie takes this very seriously," Sarah said.

"I'm glad. It was the rock I found that first day that kept me from leaving…and it was the reason I decided to come back."

"Trust."

Jace nodded. "It's not always easy…but when we get out of the way, God does amazing things."

The only thing left of the original homestead was a section of the stone foundation. The yellow daylilies the volunteers had planted around it were in full bloom.

A little over ten years ago, Jace had been sitting on the wall, waiting for her.

Jace's hand tightened around hers. "I'm sorry."

Sarah leaned against his shoulder. "And I'm sorry I wouldn't let Maggie tell you that I was pregnant. We're looking forward, not back, remember?"

"I remember." Jace guided Sarah toward the wall and she saw a flash of gold in the flowers. She bent down and moved the leaves aside. "Addie's golden rock. She only paints one, so finding it has become an event in itself every summer," she told him. "This one must have been hidden so well, no one found it last year."

Jace smiled.

She picked up the rock and frowned. "She didn't write a message on it."

"Maybe the other side?" Jace suggested.

Sarah turned it over and went still.

Written in a bold, upright script, were two words.

Marry Me.

Sarah's eyes flew to Jace.

Cradled in the palm of his hand was a small velvet box.

Jace saw the stunned look on Sarah's face, and it occurred to him—a little belatedly—that maybe he was rushing things a bit. But he'd already lost ten years, and was anxious to start their future together.

He'd even asked Addie's permission to propose to Sarah. Not only had she given it, his sweet, amazing daughter had instructed him on the proper way to go about it.

You have to buy a beautiful ring, Dad. And Mom's really smart, so you have to think of a way to surprise her. She might cry, but that's okay. Sometimes girls cry when they're happy. Tell her how much you love her and she'll say yes.

Jace must have gotten a deer-in-the-headlights look, because Addie had patted his shoulder and said, *I'll help.*

When she'd shown him the rock and presented her plan, Jace was pretty sure the surprise element was covered. He chose the place, though. Jace couldn't erase the memory of all the hurtful things he'd said the last morning he was at Four Arrows, but he could give Sarah a new one. A memory they could build a future on, instead of the one that had torn them apart.

"Marry me, Sarah. Please." Jace had rehearsed the proposal, but couldn't remember a single word now that Sarah's beautiful green eyes were focused on him. "You said we have to keep moving forward, but every step we take, I want to be next to you. I want us to be a family." Jace's breath hitched in his throat. "I realize some people might think we should take things slow, but I've waited ten years and—"

"Yes." Tears streamed down Sarah's cheeks. "Yes, I'll marry you."

Tears stabbed the back of Jace's eyes. Yup. Sometimes guys cried when they were happy, too.

He slipped the ring on Sarah's finger and drew her into his arms.

"I told you she'd say yes!"

Jace wrapped an arm around Addie and included her in the embrace. A moment later, she wriggled free, eyes shining as she looked at Sarah.

"Do you like the ring, Mom? Dad picked it out all by himself, but the gold rock was my idea."

"It's perfect." Sarah stretched out her hand and the diamonds winked in the sunlight.

Jace could finally breathe again.

He'd left the camp one day under the guise of running errands and gone to a jewelry store instead, but only one ring in the case caught Jace's eye. Three diamonds, set in a simple gold band. He knew Sarah would understand.

"Should we go home and celebrate?"

"With ice cream?" Addie said hopefully.

Sarah laughed.

Jace loved it when she laughed, but even more, he loved it when she looked at him the way she was looking at him now.

"For this family…is there any other way?"

Sarah was the first person to spot the lone figure standing on the shoreline when they returned to the camp.

"Who's that?" Addie had noticed her, too.

"I'm not sure." It wouldn't be the first time that a curious tourist had wandered off the beaten path and ended up at the camp. "How about I find out while you two make the sundaes?"

"Okay!" Addie tugged Jace toward the cabin and Sarah veered toward the lake.

The woman, wearing a sleeveless linen dress and sandals, stared at the water. Tall and slender, she wore her long brown hair woven into a neat braid that trailed between her shoulder blades. Even without the oversize sunglasses that shielded half of her face from view, Sarah wouldn't have recognized her.

"Hi!" Sarah called out a greeting when she was several yards away. "Can I help you?"

The woman turned toward Sarah almost reluctantly and then her eyes widened.

"Sarah?"

"Yes." Awkward. Sarah tried to match the woman's face with a name. A hazard of the job when you met hundreds of people every year.

The woman whipped off her sunglasses, revealing a pair of indigo-blue eyes, and the mystery was solved.

"Rae." Sarah couldn't believe it. "Rae Channing."

"That's me."

"I'm so sorry—"

"Don't apologize," Rae cut her off with a warm smile. "The last time you saw me, I think my hair was pink."

"Turquoise."

"Ah. Right." Rae's perfectly straight nose wrinkled. "It was a revolving color wheel then. Part of my disguise."

Sarah remembered that Rae's baggy clothing had concealed her figure as effectively as her eyes had concealed her thoughts.

Rae was studying her, too. Wondering, like Sarah, where life had taken them over the past ten years?

"Maggie—" Remembering how the news about Maggie's death had shaken Jace, she wasn't sure how to tell Rae.

"I heard." Rae's smile faded. "But I got a postcard in the mail and I...I couldn't ignore it. Was it from you?"

Sarah glanced at the cabin. "Why don't we go somewhere that we can talk?"

And Sarah wanted Jace to be part of the conversation, too.

Rae cast another look at the lake and nodded almost reluctantly.

Jace and Addie stood at the counter, lining bowls with every possible topping a person could put on an ice cream sundae.

"Just in time," Jace said without looking up. "The ice cream is starting to melt."

"Jace?" Rae laughed. "I knew you'd stay."

Jace turned around, slowly. The confusion in his eyes told Sarah she wasn't the only one who'd failed to recognize the only girl in the trio Maggie had invited to Four Arrows.

He dropped the spoon on the counter and padded into the living room. Studied her a moment, and then said, "Rae?"

Addie, who'd followed him, gasped. "The girl with the mermaid hair!"

Rae looked amused by the description. "Not the statement I was going for at the time, but I like it."

"You got the postcard I sent!"

"*You* sent it?" Rae glanced at Sarah and Jace.

"We better eat the ice cream first," he said. "This conversation could take a while."

They took the bowls out to the patio, and Rae perched on the edge of a wicker chair. Addie finished first and asked if she could go to the barn to visit Star.

"I'm glad you came." She grinned at Rae. "My dad got here first, but we're still waiting for Ian."

Sarah released a slow breath when Addie dashed away.

Rae's eyes mirrored her confusion as her gaze bounced between Sarah and Jace. "First?"

"Long story." Jace took Sarah's hand and gave it a reassuring squeeze. "It took me ten years to figure out what you did that summer. Addie's postcard brought me back, too, but I'm here to stay."

"The note on the postcard said you needed help." Rae set her bowl down.

Sarah winced. "There are some…gaps…that need filling, but please, don't feel obligated in any way. We're trusting God to provide what we need."

A shadow skimmed through Rae's eyes.

"The postcards were my idea," she said simply. "What kind of gaps?"

Sarah gave in. "Mrs. Hoffman has supervised the cafeteria for years, but she isn't available this summer, so we need someone to oversee the cafeteria and special events."

Rae was staring at Sarah in disbelief.

"I know…it's a lot. It's not a paid position, either," Sarah added quickly. "We'd never expect you to—"

A cell phone began to ring in Rae's purse. She fished it out and frowned at the screen. "Duty calls." She rose to her feet. "I'm sorry it's taken me so long to respond to Addie's card, but this is the first day I've taken off in five years."

Sarah felt a pinch of guilt. "I'm sorry—"

"Don't be. I wanted to see Four Arrows again." A smile rustled at the corners of Rae's lips. "I remember Mrs. Hoffman. She let me hide out in the kitchen and I learned a lot from her. It's one of the reasons I became a chef."

"A chef," Jace repeated.

"It'll take some time to work out a few wrinkles, but I should be back in a couple of days."

"You're coming back?" Sarah choked out.

"Right now, Four Arrows needs me more than the restaurant does, so you and I will come up with a plan. When I gave that card to Maggie, I meant it…and I never break a promise." Rae's smile bloomed. "Tell Addie I look forward to seeing her again."

After she'd left, Sarah looked at Jace. He appeared as shell-shocked as she was.

"What just happened?" she whispered.

"I think… Addie prayed big."

"Jace… Rae is a chef. A *chef*." Sarah laughed and wiped away a tear that leaked from her eye. "Maggie always said that God has a sense of humor."

"I remember something else she said." Jace pulled Sarah into his arms.

"What?" She leaned against him, felt the steady beat of his heart.

"Are you ready for an adventure?"

Sarah smiled up at Jace. Their lives had taken different paths, and yet here they were, together.

"I can't wait."

* * * * *

Dear Reader,

While I was growing up, a week at camp was the highlight of my summer vacation. Nightly bonfires and sing-alongs. Long hikes and splashing in the lake. Making new friends. I'd return home with a sunburn, some type of creation fashioned from wooden craft sticks and so many stories to tell my family.

The time was short and yet it had such an impact on my life. Not only did I learn about God and enjoy the beauty of His creation, I learned some things about myself, too. Like, I'm pretty good at archery!

Reliving all those sweet memories made writing Sarah and Jace's story even more fun. If you enjoyed your first visit to Four Arrows, I'd love to hear from you. Drop by my website at kathrynspringer.com (and sign up for my newsletter while you're there!) or follow me on Instagram at kathrynspringerauthor.

Joy in the journey,
Kathryn

Harlequin Reader Service

Enjoyed your book?

Try the perfect subscription for Romance readers and get more great books like this delivered right to your door.

See why over 10+ million readers have tried Harlequin Reader Service.

Start with a Free Welcome Collection with free books and a gift—valued over $20.

Choose any series in print or ebook. See website for details and order today:

TryReaderService.com/subscriptions

RSBPA2409